The Ghosts of Idlewood

Book One

Idlewood Series

By M.L. Bullock

62—15

Dedication

This book is dedicated to Kim Heights, Joyce Jividen and
Julie Summers. I will never forget my friends,
the girls of summer.

TALLULAH

And when this body dies, shall I with thee
Pass into brute, or bird, or wood, or stone,
Until refreshed the vital spark shall be,
And into human form again we run,—
Thus changing ever till the work is done?
And when this universe has passed away,
And earth lies like a mist without a sun,
What semblance shall I wear of perished clay
Beneath th' effulgent light of that unending day?

And shall I recognize the different beings then
Through which my fleeting essence shall have pass'd,
And understand them all? as, with the ken
Of angel thought, my curious eye is cast
Along the varied chain from first to last,—
Link after link, now glittering and now gone,—
Yet bound together in one being fast,
And ever reaching upwards, one by one,
From cradled earth to God's eternal throne?

Excerpt from TALLULAH

General Henry Rootes Jackson, 1850

Prologue – Percy

Mobile, Alabama
1870

Aubrey burrowed into Percy's shoulder as they huddled together in the carriage that climbed the steep drive to Idlewood. The earlier rain made the red dirt road slick, and the wheels of the carriage made an unpleasant sucking noise as they rolled through the mud toward his family home. The air felt clean and surprisingly cold. It was rare to experience such a cold snap before January. They could have come home last night, for they were near enough to do so when they stepped off the train. But after all this time, Percy wanted to see the house in the bright light of day. He wanted his new wife to see Idlewood's beauty and love it, love it like he did. And he wanted to make this a fresh start. He had a new life now. He could leave the shadows of the past behind and step into the light with Aubrey by his side. She brought sunshine into his dreary world, and she would do the same for his entire family.

It was November. Percy had been gone for two months—two whole months away from Idlewood. He could hardly believe he had managed it, but he enjoyed the adventures of new marriage. Aubrey was a modestly pretty girl who was completely devoted to him and seemed to genuinely love him. He had been lucky in that regard. She was amiable and something of an intellect, which he appreciated, but after just one week of travel he'd grown weary of the constantly changing surroundings and of her need to talk quite so much.

He daydreamed as his wife chattered on about one thing and another; in his head he was at Idlewood. He might be walking to the pond to fish or strolling through the wild patch of sage that grew thick and pungent behind the old barn. He had memorized every book title in the study and knew where to find even the least-read selections like *Traveler's Descent* by Morgan Longwood. How he hated that book!

But more than anything, he missed Tallulah.

It had been two weeks since his twin sister had written him, although she'd been faithful to do so when he'd first departed. How she'd cried while he packed his trunk and prepared for the journey he would take without her. "This isn't what you promised, Percy. This is not the way it should be!" He had consoled her with promises of gifts and letters until finally she'd quit crying and helped him arrange his things.

Hansel and Gretel.

That's what their mother used to call them, when she remembered to notice them. Ann Ferguson spent all her time spying on their father, convinced he was up to mischief in the barn with the neighbors or in some other part of the county with someone else, although he never was. Their father would never have behaved the way their mother feared he did, but one would have had a devil of a time convincing her of that. As far as their mother was concerned, Charles Ferguson was a handsome and desirable catch despite the fact that he had been married to her for nearly twenty years, had gout occasionally and had a generally dark disposition.

Hansel and Gretel.

Percy fussed about the moniker, but secretly, he liked it. It tied him and Tallulah together, for they had always been together. Even the night *the bad thing* happened. They were together then, holding one another. That was before the other children came along. Not that they didn't love them. But they *were* Hansel and Gretel.

During these weeks of travel, Percy had read and reread each correspondence from his sister, and stayed up all hours himself writing her long descriptive paragraphs detailing all that he'd seen, tasted or smelled that day. Aubrey complained that he would succumb to eyestrain, but he assured her that he could see just as well by candlelight as he could by the light of day.

Tallulah's first letter had been waiting for him when he checked in at the Burfield Hotel in Atlanta. Each correspondence he treated like a welcoming breadcrumb that would lead him along his journey and then home again. Tallulah's letters were bits of home; she would know that he needed them, and he savored them all along the way. But then, on the return trip to that same hotel, he arrived and there was nothing waiting for him—not even a letter from his father. Only the expected financial dispensation intended to be used on frivolous gifts for his wife and whatever experiences their hearts desired. All their expenses had been covered by his father. Percy had purchased his wife a set of china with pink and lavender flowers and had it sent home to Idlewood. He bought her hats, dresses, parasols and even a small white puppy she named Glad. The couple had traveled as far as Virginia and spent time on glassy Lake Moomaw in the Shenandoah Valley. Unfortunately, they'd lost Glad in the woods near the lake, and Aubrey had mourned him for all of two hours. However, to make her smile again he promised her another dog when they arrived home. A good breed, perhaps a greyhound. She had been satisfied with his thoughtfulness.

Aubrey fell in love with the lake cabin and hinted that she would not be opposed to making the valley home. Percy smiled good-naturedly, but he wouldn't even entertain the idea. No way would he ever abandon Tallulah or permanently leave Idlewood, although he suspected his father would support his decision to do so.

Charles Ferguson believed that a man should make his own way in the world. A family man should be a force of nature—strong, determined and ever eager to promote the welfare of those he had a responsibility to care for. Idlewood had survived the war because his father had wisely invested the family fortune in overseas businesses long before the upheaval of war had begun. The Fergusons' growing fortune irked many of the Mobile County bluebloods—some even went so far as to accuse Mr. Ferguson of being a Yankee sympathizer—but his father had not stood for that. No indeed. The loudest, most vocal accuser, a Mr. Oscar Loper, had been promptly sued for slander. He lost the case, and now the Ferguson fortune included the Lopers' sawmill and a modest peanut farm. This new acquisition would someday be distributed to one of the Ferguson children. No further accusations were made against his family and all was well, as far as the family's standing in society went.

Fortunately for Percy, he had been too young to go to war. And unlike some of his friends, he did not feel as if he had missed out on anything. War had devastated the nation. He was glad he had not contributed to the destruction or spilled any blood.

At least not in the War.

As the couple rounded the hilltop and the carriage pulled in front of the house, Percy knew something was wrong. His unease increased as he noticed that only a few familiar servants greeted him. No members of his family stood on the porch as he expected them to, and he knew that his siblings would have heard his carriage. They would have known he was on the way; surely they had received his message last night. Yet they were not there to greet him. Percy sat stiffly in the seat for a few seconds trying to collect himself. Then he noticed the wide black ribbons hanging from the door knocker—a sudden breeze sent them sailing and fluttering as if they had a life of their own. He hadn't seen those ribbons for many years. The last time had been when his grandfather Lane Ferguson died while stoking the fire in the Great Room.

And only once before that.

Percy's heart fell. He set his square jaw and chiseled face and stepped out of the carriage. He straightened his jacket and helped his wife navigate the narrow metal step. She slid her arm through his and stared up at him with wide dark eyes.

Without a word, he led her up the stairs. And although he only glanced at her, he could see that Aubrey's face was very pale, as white as the columns of Idlewood. He should probably have inquired about her health, for that would have been the polite thing to do, but he just couldn't muster one more polite thing at the moment. It was all he could do to walk up the painted steps at a presentable pace. But he did the polite thing. He always would because she needed him. Aubrey was his first priority now, according to the law. Percy wanted to spring ahead of her, run inside the house as he had when he was a child and learn the reason for the black ribbons, but duty forced him to walk slowly and treat his wife with care. She too knew something was amiss, but he ignored her questioning eyes.

Mrs. Potts, the housekeeper, knew every detail of what was going on, but he couldn't bring himself to question her. It was obvious she had been crying that morning. Her puffy pink face appeared even puffier, and her white cap shook and rested crooked. That struck him as extremely odd. She wrung her hands and then remembered herself and left them stiffly at her side.

"Mrs. Potts," he said in a quiet voice.

"I am so happy that you are here, Mister Percy. Your mother will be glad you are home at last. And I am happy to see you looking so well, Mrs. Ferguson."

So it's my father, then, he reasoned to himself. *Something has happened to Father.*

"Same to you, Mrs. Potts," Aubrey said politely. "I am happy to see you again."

With a final clip of his chin, Percy led Aubrey through the open doors of the house. He did not want to admit that his presumption about the death of his father left him feeling peaceful. His father's death would make sense. He was getting on in years and worked far too much. Not that he hated his father. Percy respected him, but it was the kind of respect that all sons of larger-than-life fathers carried. Fathers should be loved from a distance, not like sisters or mothers. They were to be respected—revered, even. His father would not have approved of him crying like a girl at his passing. He jutted out his chin even more. It would be Percy's time to be the man of the house, to take care of his mother and siblings. At least until Michael was old enough to help him manage things. And there was Mr. Quigley, the family attorney, who was more like an uncle than a legal consultant. Yes, he could do this. It was time to be strong for Mother and Tallulah and Aubrey and Bridget and Dot. They walked through the foyer; nothing had changed here. The square-topped Chesterfield table held a seasonal arrangement of fall flowers, burgundy candles and cheery pumpkins. They walked past the wide staircase that took up most of the room and through the arched doorway leading to the gallery at the back of the house. This was where his father's body would be laid out, just as his grandfather's had been.

And the one before that.

Yes, he could hear his mother crying softly now. *No, that was not Mother. That was Bridget. How odd that she would sound so grown.* Aubrey glanced up at him for comfort. He could offer none. He felt her grip tighten on his arm. The walls of the hallway had been freshly painted; the place appeared spotless, as it always did. Father insisted on neatness. That was a standard for the house that Percy intended to continue.

He pushed the door open and walked through the anteroom into the gallery. The doors were slid back so he could take in the wide view of the somber party gathered there. The curtains were pulled back, and Percy's eyes fell on the great gold mirror that hung at the end of the gallery. It had been covered with black cloth to prevent mourners from peeping at their own reflection. It was the Scottish way—and make no mistake, the Fergusons were Scottish, although their family had been in Mobile for nearly fifty years now. The family motto, *Dulcius Ex Asperis* or "sweeter after difficulties," was plainly emblazoned in gold paint over the doorway of this very room. Percy felt Aubrey pause in the doorway. He did not drag her on or compel her to attend him. In fact, he felt relieved to be free of her grasp, at least for a moment. He released her arm gently, allowing her to linger in the doorway as he took a few more steps into the room. All eyes were upon him, but his light blue eyes were on the wooden coffin. The pedestal was draped in black and made the disturbing scene all the more like a play, one of Bridget's plays, which were always depressing and sentimental if not bordering on pagan and evil.

No, it had not been Bridget crying but Dot. The youngest of the Ferguson clan.

*One step, two steps…*on he went, his sorrow deepening as his realization of the horrible truth grew with every step.

He counted the faces as he made his way to the burnished wooden box. Percy acknowledged no one but just stared at them blankly. There they were, each and every one present, except the one he longed to see. Except she *was* there, tidily tucked in a box made to fit her perfect frame. He spied the glint of bright blond hair, the yellow dress and pale bare toes that peeked out from under the ribboned dress hem at the end of the box. Surrounding her resting figure was his family. His father stood beside his brother, Michael, near her head. His brother's hand rested upon his mother's shoulder as if to claim her. Their mother smothered her cries in a handkerchief, one of the new ones his twin had embroidered the month before he left. Bridget was there, her wild brown hair twisted into a neat wreath around her head. Standing close to her but not too close was Dot, whom everyone else called Trinket; her six-year old face appeared as pinched and as pale as Aubrey's. Everyone was here.

Including Tallulah.

Tallulah's hands were folded across her chest, a peace lily perched between her fingers as if she had picked it to take with her. He knew for a fact she would never have picked a lily for any occasion. She loved roses and honeysuckle.

For a moment, he thought this might be some horrible joke. A horrid prank orchestrated by Bridget, who had a mind for such things. He stood ten feet away now. Yes, that must be it. He hesitated as he stared at Bridget, but she didn't speak or smile. She merely stared at Tallulah as if she too hoped she would leap out of the box. Frozen in his tracks now, he stared at Tallulah's chest to see if it would rise and fall. There was nothing to see. No breath of life present. She could not be dead, could she? Not death. Surely not. Another glance at Bridget told him this was not a prank, not a twisted joke. This was a nightmare come true.

Behind him he heard people gathering, whispering. Mrs. Potts must have sent notice to the neighbors; he could hear the loud voice of Mr. Langley, the closest neighbor to Idlewood. Percy edged forward a bit more. Candles were lit around Tallulah's face, although there was really no need for them. Diffused natural light poured in through the rectangular windows. He continued to study her perfect face. No eyelid moved, and the blue vein in her neck did not throb with life. No shifting of the hands.

Yes. Tallulah was dead. He would never hear her laughter or her pleasant voice again. He would never pat her hand

and assure her that all would be well. For in truth it would not be. Nothing would be well again.

Then he remembered this moment.

He'd experienced this before, in a nightmare or perhaps in a moment of déjà vu, as the French called it. He had seen this all before, not once but several times. The scene had been exactly the same too. He wore the same blue suit with the matching blue silk tie. The tie clip with the wolf's head was a wedding gift from Aubrey, purchased on their last stop before returning home. He remembered the dream, the anguished look on his mother's face, the purifying smell of paint, the cloudy sky, the biting temperature.

And he remembered seeing Tallulah in her yellow dress with the ruffles at the sleeves. Her long, wavy blond hair perfectly cinched back from her face in ivory barrettes. She looked like an angel. An angel with a red raw stripe about her petite neck.

Yes, he remembered it all perfectly now.

And he screamed.

Chapter One—Carrie Jo

I honked the horn like a crazy person hoping to get the attention of the driver ahead of me. The light was green, and had been for a while, but this jerk was too busy staring at his cell phone to actually drive. "Not the day for this, buddy," I complained from behind the wheel. Baby AJ gurgled in the back seat, and I immediately felt guilty. My son deserved a mom who had it together, who didn't bark at distracted drivers, who didn't look like she'd just rolled out of a barn. I couldn't see him in his rear-facing car seat, but as always he sounded happy and playful. Waking up every two hours last night didn't bother him, not one single bit. Me, however? I was a whole 'nother story, as Detra Ann liked to say.

According to the rearview mirror I needed to sleep for about a year or stock up on some high-end concealer. I could also plainly see that the eyeliner under my left eye was as crooked as all get-out, and I'd completely forgotten lipstick. My wild hair was long overdue for a trim—my messy bun didn't look too professional, but I kept missing my hair appointments. I always found an excuse to skip them. Since the arrival of my son, I was perpetually out of sorts.

Did I mention I was sleep-deprived? Not good for a "dream catcher."

And when was the last time I'd had a dream? Gosh, I couldn't even remember.

Ashland was gone so much lately—he'd been traveling, liquidating assets, trying to stop the financial bleeding. This last stretch he'd been gone nearly a week, and I was beginning to feel like a single parent. This morning, I woke up late and didn't have the time or brains to put any effort into my wardrobe; thus the wearing of Old Reliable—my black pantsuit from college. I suddenly found myself wishing my mother would come back to Mobile. I missed her, which was weird since we'd not been that close before.

I sighed as the Camry driver in front of me rolled to another stop and began tapping on his phone. Too many lights on Government Street. The frequent stops had never bothered me before, but life with a baby gave you a new perspective on things.

Good Lord, I was impatient! When was the last time I took a few minutes just to appreciate the mossy oaks that lined Government Street? The vintage gas lamps and friendly pedestrians? Well, it wouldn't be today. I didn't have time to stare out the window anymore. I missed that luxury. I'd spent the past six months running late and missing the party altogether. I took a deep breath and tapped on the steering wheel impatiently. I flipped on some soft jazz and eased through the light when it changed. Thankfully I didn't have to remind the guy ahead of me again.

Two big things were happening today. I would finally begin the major project at Idlewood, and Ashland James Junior was headed off for his first day at day care. I couldn't decide which I was more nervous about. No, that wasn't true. It was definitely the latter. For the past few months, the baby and I had gotten quite comfortable hanging out around the house and visiting the park at Cadillac Square while Ashland "jet-setted" around the Gulf Coast with Libby Stevenson. I admired his work ethic, and I absolutely trusted him (*I did trust him, right?*), but sometimes I wished he'd stop trying to rescue everyone else and just rescue me.

Funny how the thing you love the most about someone can also be the thing that drives you absolutely bonkers.

"How you doing back there, little man?" AJ sputtered happily, and I could tell by the jangling of his car seat toy that he was having a good old time. I passed Carlen Street. It was a one-way, so I had to make the block to get to AJ's day care over off Dauphin. "Almost there!" I said more brightly than I actually felt.

A few turns and two lights later, we were pulling into Small Steps Daycare. They'd come highly recommended by Aimee, Detra Ann's new shop assistant. I took a peek at the facility, "interviewed" the owner and left feeling good about it all. But that was before I had to drop off my son there.

"Hi, Carrie Jo—and good morning, Ashland! You ready to play?" That was Jessica, AJ's new pal and the facility's supervisor. He'd met her last week and seemed to like her. As instructed, I didn't get out of the car when I arrived. Jessica explained that it made the transition easier if parents stayed in the car, but she understood if I wanted to come inside the first few times. I followed her suggestion and gripped the steering wheel like I was dying. Letting go was harder than I imagined. Jessica and her helper removed the baby and his diaper bag and closed the door behind them. The sound nearly broke my heart. What kind of mother was I, giving my baby to strangers? Never mind the fact that I could watch him the whole time from the computer in my office. All the classrooms at Small Steps had "Mommy Cams."

I rolled down the window, uncaring about the line forming behind me.

"And you have my number, right? If you need anything at all, anything, just holler at me. Okay? I'm just like two streets over."

"We will, Mommy. Have a good day! See you at noon!"

"Okay," I said, swallowing tears as the car rolled to the end of the driveway. I took a deep breath and turned back onto busy Dauphin Street. Even though it was after eight o'clock, cars were everywhere. This was an old area that had seen quite a bit of revitalization the past few years. I was happy that my husband and I had contributed to that in some way. Seven Sisters was only a few blocks away— my first house renovation in this area...and my first ever. To say that it was a life-changing experience would be an understatement. And even though I hadn't been back to the plantation-turned-museum in over six months, it held a special place in my heart for more reasons than I could count.

Oh, baby AJ. What am I doing leaving you? Life is too precarious to let the ones you love go unprotected!

I sniffed against a threatening onset of Mommy-guilt. I hadn't made it to Carlen Street before the tears threatened to reappear. As if my husband read my mind, my phone rang and his handsome face appeared on the screen. I sighed with relief and pulled the car into a rare empty parking spot on Dauphin Street before answering. I was only two driveways from Idlewood, but I didn't want Desmond Taylor seeing me cry if he made an unscheduled visit. Which he was likely to do.

"Good morning, gorgeous. How did our boy do this morning?"

"Better than Mommy, I'm afraid."

He laughed, but not in a mocking way. As always, he was a thoughtful man. *Now, if he'd just come home so I could sleep through the night!* "Having second thoughts, babe?"

I leaned my head against the seat back for a second before answering. "No, I don't think so. I mean, not really. Why? Do you think I should go back and get him?"

His patient voice poured through the phone like soothing honey. "CJ, he's going to be fine. The place has a stellar reputation. We were lucky to get him in there, and you need this. You need a project, something you can sink your teeth into. Not to mention we can use the money, although I expect that is going to turn around soon. I got an offer on the house in New Orleans."

"That's great, Ashland. I hate to see you sell another one of your properties."

"Yeah, but it's got to be done. And since I haven't told you this today, I love you, Carrie Jo."

"I love you too, Ashland. Now come home. Like, today."

"I'm on it. I'll be home this evening."

I paused, not sure what to say to him. I just knew I didn't want the conversation to end.

"You okay?"

I shook my head as if he could see me. "Not really, no."

"Don't overthink this. Get back to doing what you love, CJ. Our son will be fine. He's in good hands. You know that.

You can't run from who you are, any more than I can. Get started."

"I know, I know. And I know I'm darn lucky that Desmond Taylor waited around for me and didn't go with someone else for this project."

I could hear the smile in his voice. "That's not what I meant. But yes, he is lucky to have you in the lead role on this."

"Well, what did you mean, then?" I sat up now and frowned at myself in the rearview mirror. That reminded me—I needed to fix my eyeliner pronto. I rubbed at the crooked line, which only made it look worse.

"This isn't criticism. So please don't take it that way. But has it ever occurred to you that you've been avoiding going back to work because you're afraid? Maybe all that you experienced at Seven Sisters traumatized you more than you realize. I think you might be letting fear get the best of you, Carrie Jo."

I stared at the phone for a moment and then put my ear back to the speaker.

"Are you there? Did I lose you?" he asked innocently.

"Yeah, I'm here. What kind of cockamamie theory is that?" I heard a woman talking in the background. Sounded like Libby. That made my blood boil even more. Here I was, struggling to keep it all together, and he was gallivanting around New Orleans with his school chum turned attorney. How convenient! "Is that some theory you and Libby came up with together? I hope I'm not the sole subject of conversation between you two." *Wow! Where did that come from?*

Had to be the hormones! Oh good God! Even though my thoughts were reasonable and my mind was telling me to shut up, my mouth wasn't having any of it. It kept on rolling. Ashland tried to speak, but I cut him off right away. I wasn't in the mood for his reasonable attitude or his amateur psychologist diagnosis this morning. "You know what, Ashland? I'm not afraid of a dang thing! You're the chicken here! I've been doing all the parenting, making all the decisions—not sleeping! How about *you* come home and change a few diapers and enjoy some of AJ's midnight feedings and then talk to me about being afraid. Afraid. That's a joke. I don't have the energy to be afraid."

"Whoa, CJ. I asked you not to take what I said as criticism. And for the record, I don't talk about..."

"I've got to go, Ashland. I'm late already."

"We can't end our conversation like this, CJ. I was only trying to help."

He was being so kind, and I was acting like a total ass. I felt my heart melt. I knew I'd been wrong, but before I could apologize I heard Libby's voice again in the background. Calling my husband.

"Ashland! You ready?"

Probably perfectly innocent, but I was already so angry at him it didn't matter. I needed to end this conversation before things got more heated. "Goodbye, Ashland." I hung up the phone and threw it in my purse. I put the car in drive, looked down the street, saw no cars coming and wheeled out onto Carlen. Dang it!

Time to put my game face on. If I hadn't felt like doing so before, I did now. If for no other reason than to prove to him that I *could* do this—and that I wasn't afraid or any such nonsense. Despite whatever theory he might have, I was more than capable of making this happen. I pulled my BMW into the driveway of Idlewood and climbed the steep hill. I'd been here before over six months ago, but not much had changed. I'd forgotten how steep the driveway was—that was something we might have to address going forward. I eased up the rest of the way, put the car in park and sat staring at the broken old home. An upstairs window was broken now. Might be some water damage inside. Wait...was someone up there? Then I saw Rachel's car. She'd beaten me to the punch.

I turned off the car and grabbed my purse and briefcase. I slid my sunglasses to the top of my head and took a good look at the front facade. She had good bones but definitely needed some love. I looked at my watch. I had a few hours to get started; baby AJ would be in day care for only half-days today and next week. I had insisted on that. I thought easing into a longer schedule would be easier on him—and me.

Idlewood was built on a small hill, which made the Greek revival home appear even larger. Some parts of the property looked good, like the brick walkway that led to the front steps. The four large oak trees that lined the walkway were in good shape too, if in need of a good trim. Concrete lions lined the front steps, but many of them were hidden from view, wrapped in green vines and other debris. There were twelve windows on the front of the house; eight of those were full-length windows complete with green shutters. The second floor had a balcony that extended around the entire house, but the floors were spongy and needed to be replaced in some areas. The columns had damage, and two needed replacing. All the windows upstairs would need to be replaced; the warped glass and missing shingles made the grand old home appear forlorn, forgotten, like a toothless old belle abandoned by her beau a very long time ago.

Most people probably didn't think about strange things like this, but I felt that some old homes had their own personalities. And it was my job to figure out this house's personality and let it shine through.

This section of Carlen Street towered over nearby Hunter Avenue. Back in the early 1800s, when Idlewood was first built, there was nothing else in this area. It was used as a working plantation by the McClellans, the builders of the home. They grew peanuts and allowed sharecroppers to grow and pick cotton during certain times of the year. Old Mr. McClellan was making money, according to the county records, but he'd gotten very ill and sold the place to his friend and fellow Scotsman Lane Ferguson. The house was a few years older than Seven Sisters. Both were massive properties in their day, and it was a rare thing to have two such homes so close together. During Calpurnia's time, Idlewood wasn't lived in year-round. The Ferguson-Mays family had another home on the other side of Mobile Bay.

After the last of the Fergusons died, it changed hands frequently, and then the house stood empty for many years until the Taylors bought it. The Taylors were related to those Fergusons somehow (that wasn't quite clear to me yet), and Desmond Taylor—at the urging of his wife and the Historical Society—was keen to make the house something special again. A showplace for the community to enjoy and rent for balls, weddings and who knew what else. Who could blame him?

I sighed as I took in the view one last time before I went to work. I closed my eyes and tried to imagine the place like it would be. Although it was quite different from Seven Sisters, it would be just as lovely, of that I had no doubt. There should be laughter here. *There hasn't been much of that. I can feel the sadness.* I shivered at that thought but refused to acknowledge any fear. Ashland was wrong. Dead wrong. I hadn't been stalling for time. The idea of restoring the place to an honorable position in Mobile thrilled me. I decided I'd begin this new journey with a walk-around of the property to get the lay of the land.

And despite what Ashland thought, I wasn't afraid. Not one little bit.

Heck no, I wasn't afraid!

Maybe I should have been.

Chapter Two—Rachel

I arrived at Idlewood at seven o'clock thinking I'd have plenty of time to mark the doors with taped signs before the various contractors arrived. There was no electricity, so I wasn't sure what the workmen would actually accomplish today. I'd dressed down this morning in worn blue jeans and a long-sleeved t-shirt. It just felt like that kind of day. The house smelled stale, and it was cool but not freezing. We'd enjoyed a mild February this year, but like they say, "If you don't like the weather in Mobile, just wait a few minutes."

I really hated February. It was "the month of love," and this year I wasn't feeling much like celebrating. I'd given Chip the heave-ho for good right after Christmas, and our friendship hadn't survived the breakup. I hated that because I really did like him as a person, even if he could be narrow-minded about spiritual subjects. I hadn't been seeing anyone, but I was almost ready to get back into the dating game. Almost.

I changed out the batteries in my camera before beginning to document the house. Carrie Jo liked having before, during and after shots of every room.

According to the planning sheet Carrie Jo and I developed last month, all the stage one doors were marked. On her jobs, CJ orchestrated everything: what rooms got painted first, where the computers would go, which room we would store supplies in, that sort of thing. I also put no-entry signs on rooms that weren't safe or were off-limits to curious workers. The home was mostly empty, but there were some pricy mantelpieces and other components that would fetch a fair price if you knew where to unload stolen items such as high-end antiques. Surprisingly, many people did.

I'd start the pictures on the top floor and work my way down. I peeked out the front door quickly to see if CJ was here. No sign of her yet, which wasn't like her at all. She was usually the early bird. I smiled, feeling good that Carrie Jo trusted me enough to give me the keys to this grand old place. There were three floors, although the attic space wasn't a real priority for our project. The windows would be changed, the floors and roof inspected, but not a lot of cosmetic changes were planned for up there beyond that. We'd prepare it for future storage of seasonal decorations and miscellaneous supplies. Seemed a waste to me. I liked the attic; it was roomy, like an amazing loft apartment. But it was no surprise I was drawn to it—when I was a kid, I practically lived in my tree house.

I stuffed my cell phone in my pocket and jogged up the wide staircase in the foyer. I could hear birds chirping upstairs; they probably flew in through a broken window. There were quite a few of them from the sound of it. Since I hadn't labeled any doors upstairs or in the attic, I hadn't had the opportunity to explore much up there. It felt strangely exhilarating to do so all by myself. The first flight of stairs appeared safe, but I took my time on the next two. Water damage wasn't always easy to spot, and I had no desire to fall through a weak floor. When I reached the top of the stairs to the attic, I turned the knob and was surprised to find it locked.

"What?" I twisted it again and leaned against the door this time, but it wouldn't move. I didn't see a keyhole, so that meant it wasn't locked after all. I supposed it was merely stuck, the wood probably swollen from moisture. "Rats," I said. I set my jaw and tried one last time. The third time must have been the charm because it opened freely, as if it hadn't given me a world of problems before. I nearly fell as it gave way, laughing at myself as I regained my balance quickly. I reached for my camera and flipped it to the video setting. I panned the room to record the contents. There were quite a few old trunks, boxes and even the obligatory dressmaker's dummy. It was a nerd girl historian's dream come true.

Like an amateur documentarian, I spoke to the camera: "Maiden voyage into the attic at Idlewood. Today is February 4th. This is Rachel Kowalski recording."

Rachel Kowalski recording, something whispered back. My back straightened, and the fine hairs on my arms lifted as if to alert me to the presence of someone or something unseen.

I froze and said, "Hello?" I was happy to hear my voice and my voice alone echo back to me.

Hello?

I chuckled at myself and began inching my way around the room. Even though I knew it was me now, the echo wasn't pleasant so I didn't speak again, I just panned and zoomed until I'd recorded everything I thought would be important, including some interesting antiques that we might be able to use during the final staging. I panned up to the ceiling and zoomed into a suspected weak spot in the corner of the room behind a stack of metal spires that came from goodness knew where. Thankfully the light in here was pretty good; the video wouldn't be too dark or grainy.

The front side of the house had plenty of attic windows, and they weren't those useless portals you sometimes saw. No, at one point, someone could have very well lived in this space. Even during the summer, a few of these open windows would have given the residents plenty of cross-ventilation. Of course, as Gran was fond of saying, "There ain't nothin' like good ol' AC." She grew up way out in the country, and she often regaled my cousins and me with tales about life without electricity and running water. She was a hoot. I didn't always believe the things she told me, but I knew that she meant well. I appreciated how far she'd brought us all. How much she'd done for Mom and me when Dad split.

Unlike some kids, I was glad to see my dad leave. He was the world's biggest jerk, and that was never going to change. And when Mom decided to begin using her maiden name again, I had demanded to be allowed to do the same. It took some legal wrangling, but Joe Rogers didn't give a damn. Didn't bother him at all. So now, Gran, Mom and I were the three Kowalskis. We were a tight little family, and I liked it that way.

I walked to one of the windows, flipped the camera back on and filmed the driveway from this amazing vantage point. Panning the camera to the right, I got a good shot of the overgrown lot the house stood on. It looked like a jungle down there, with way too many wild sticker vines to even consider taking a tour of the limited grounds. Still no sign of Carrie Jo, unless she parked up close to the house; the roof of the balcony below me blocked my view of that part of the driveway.

I stood on tiptoe, but it didn't do a bit of good. I wasn't that tall to begin with. I glanced at my watch. Yeah, I'd better get downstairs. Carrie Jo wouldn't be much longer. I walked back to the door, promising myself that I'd come back up on my lunch break to plunder the chests. The things people hid away were always revealing and informative about who they were. And if any of these boxes and things belonged to the Fergusons, Carrie Jo would be tickled pink. I must have stirred up the thick layer of dust that coated the room because I sneezed without any warning at all. I waited for the echo and frowned when it didn't come. *Now that's odd. Must be the weird acoustics in here.*

I stepped out into the hall and felt compelled to close the door behind me. In fact, I couldn't close it fast enough. I heard the voice again, and it wasn't my voice. I hadn't said a word. The voice belonged to someone much younger.

And probably much deader.

My hand froze on the doorknob as I tried to release it. Something didn't want to let me go.

Rachel Kowalski…recording…

I tugged with all my might, and with a desperate, muffled scream, the invisible force let go of my hand and I broke free. I fell backwards onto the dirty floor. I didn't waste time trying to figure out if anything was broken. I scrambled to my feet and scurried down the stairs like my pants were on fire. I heard a voice calling me from the bottom floor. It was a voice I knew. A living voice.

"Rachel? You up there?"

Oh God, thank you, God!

"Yes! I'm coming!" I said as I barreled down the last flight of stairs. Carrie Jo stood in the foyer looking at me questioningly.

"You okay?" She laughed nervously, like she was half ready to run too. I remembered a t-shirt I owned: *Paranormal Investigator: If You See Me Running, Run Faster.* I'd probably wear it tomorrow. My first instinct was to blurt it all out, tell her that something mocked me in the attic, that it grabbed my hand and scared the hell out of me. But one look at her face told me this wasn't the day for that. Carrie Jo would have made a terrible poker player.

"Um, yeah. Just wanted to be here when you got here. Did some filming in the attic, but I haven't finished the rest of the house yet. Want to walk with me?"

"Sure." She smiled and set her purse and briefcase down on the only table available. "Let's do this. It's day one, and we've got a long way to go."

"Hey, that would be great to put on video. What do you say? Should we do this video diary up right?" *Yes, please give me something normal to do.*

She smiled nervously and fiddled with her hair. "I don't know, Rachel. I look like hell today. Baby AJ doesn't know how to sleep for longer than a few hours."

"Nonsense, you are gorgeous, CJ. If you want to do it tomorrow, I understand, but there's nothing like the first day. It's kind of magical, isn't it?" I put on my best smile. It was obvious my boss needed some cheering.

"No, you're right. It's a great idea. We should do it now, but give me two minutes to put my lipstick on. I could at least do that. If I can remember where there's a bathroom."

"Oh, yeah. That reminds me. No power, no water. I think we'll be spending today waiting on service trucks."

"Great. I'll just use this." She dug in her purse and found her lipstick and walked to the nearest window.

I fiddled with my camera to cue it up for Carrie Jo's bit. I played back the video a few seconds to make sure I didn't record over anything important.

Rachel Kowalski…recording.

"Oh my God!" I said aloud, not thinking that CJ could hear me.

"What is it? Lose your footage?" she called over her shoulder.

"No, not exactly." I turned the volume down and played it again.

Rachel Kowalski…recording.

I couldn't believe it. I had managed to record a ghost's voice—or something. I'd have to listen to it again later, when my skin wasn't trying to crawl off my body.

So it was true, then! I had always heard these old houses were often home to spirits but had never thought much about it. My mother and aunts were going to get a kick out of this. Unlike some families, mine believed in and embraced the supernatural world. To hear my grandmother tell it, all Kowalskis were spiritual people, but some were late bloomers. Like me. I'd never seen or heard anything growing up. Now I was hearing things. Freaky to think that I would be excited about it.

"Okay, how do I look?"

She'd taken her hair down and tidied it with her fingers. She wore perfectly applied lipstick now and even used a dab of it to brighten her cheeks. I wished I was half as pretty as she was. This wasn't the first time I'd had a twinge of jealousy working with CJ.

"Beautiful, of course. You know you could have been a model."

She laughed aloud at that. "Yeah, right."

"I'm not kidding! Come on, boss lady. We'll start outside the front door. Why don't you invite the viewer to follow you inside? Don't tell them about your plans for the house this go-around. Just point out important features, maybe some things that are unique about Idlewood. And of course throw in any history that you can remember."

"Geesh, Spielberg. Anything else?" Her mood had lightened since she'd arrived. I felt good about that. I suspected she and Ashland were fighting again. It was the new couple curse. You either broke it or it broke you. (Another Granism.) My sincere hope was that they broke it in a hurry. They were a dynamite team and had managed to survive so much already.

"Nope. Just remember to smile big. Ready?"

She hugged me. "Thank you for being you. I am so grateful to have you on my team."

For the next twenty minutes, I filmed Carrie Jo pointing excitedly at crown molding, special ceiling medallions and built-in wooden shelves. She did a great job of treating the camera like it was a good friend. By the time we finished the bottom floor, she was ready to head upstairs.

"Hold that thought, though; I have to call the water and electric folks to see what's up."

"Okay, no problem, CJ. That will give me a chance to review this real quick. In case we need to retake anything."

I rolled the camera back the full thirty minutes and saw Carrie Jo's smiling face appear in the open front doorway. "Hi! I'm Carrie Jo Jardine, and I'd like to welcome you to Idlewood, a once-beautiful old mansion in downtown Mobile, Alabama. Let's go inside and see what it looks like now." I smiled back at Carrie Jo. She absolutely forgot to use her married name. Not a problem, really; I could edit that out. I chuckled as I replayed it.

Then I heard the voice again.

Rachel Kowalski…recording.

The voice came in and out, as if it were speaking over a distorted radio channel or something, but it was clearly playing through my camera. My hair stood up again. I couldn't believe this! Something or someone wanted my attention.

I wandered to the opposite side of the room and whispered to whoever might be listening. Maybe I could reason with it. "I hear you, but please don't scare my friend. She can help you. I'll try to help you too, but no more scary stuff, okay?" I stared up the stairs and heard the sound of little feet running away, back to the attic. I even heard the door slam.

"What was that?" Carrie Jo asked, her green eyes wide with fear.

"The attic windows are open, and I must have left the door open when I came back down," I lied horribly. *That's so bad for my karma.*

"Oh, okay. Sorry to be so jumpy today. I'm just missing baby AJ. And did I tell you how tired I am?" She laughed nervously. "Ready to head upstairs now?"

"Yes, but just in case, I want to change out my cards. Just a second." It was a brand new video card, so there shouldn't be a trace of a voice on there. No one's voice should be on this one. I popped it in and put the old one in my jeans pocket. "Now I'm ready. These stairs are steady. No wonky or saggy steps. Let's film the walk-up."

"Great! Let's roll some footage. I am so excited about this now. Can't believe we didn't do this before."

"Just one thing," I advised with another smile.

"Yeah?" she said as she climbed to the landing and gave me a dopey pose.

"In the last video you called yourself Carrie Jo Jardine."

"No, I didn't. Did I?"

"Yes, but I'm sure you didn't mean anything by it, and Ashland wasn't here to hear it. I'll edit that bit out later." *I have quite a bit of editing to do, actually, and not because of Carrie Jo.*

"Let's try it again, then. Let me practice...Hi! I'm Carrie Jo *Stuart*. Yes, I'm Carrie Jo Stuart." Each time she said it, she sounded more chipper.

I grinned and gave her a thumbs-up. "Let's do this, then. Let's start with that, give your name again and tell the viewers where we are and what they'll see. Ready? I'll count you down from three."

"Cool! Okay, I'm ready."

"Three, two, one..."

"Hi, I'm Carrie Jo Stuart, and I'm here to show you the many wonderful features inside this lovely old home called Idlewood. We are currently in downtown Mobile, Alabama, right off busy Carlen Street. That's between Dauphin and Government Streets, important streets both then and now. And here in the home of Desmond and Cindy Taylor, we are finding all sorts of architectural treasures. My team and I are on the lookout for anything we can repurpose or refurbish in restoring the old home. Ready to take a look with me?"

"Cut!" I said, waving my hand. "That was perfect, and you even got your name right."

"Ha ha!" she snorted back at me. "I believe you, but before we go any further, I want to see it. If I look like hell, I don't need to be on film. I know I said I wanted a video document for this project, but that was before I had been without sleep for six months."

"No problem, boss lady. Let me rewind the video here, and you can take a look for yourself. But I'm telling you, you are worried for nothing." I smiled reassuringly. I thought I heard a service truck pull up, but I couldn't be sure. I flipped the camera to play, and Carrie Jo stood beside me to watch her video roll on the flip-out screen.

"Hi, I'm Carrie Jo Stuart, and I'm here to show you the many wonderful features inside this lovely old home called Idlewood. We are currently...*Rachel Kowalski...recording...Rachel Kowalski...recording....*" And on and on it went—the invisible child's voice spoke the words faster and faster until I set the camera down on the table and hit the power button.

Carrie Jo stared at the camera and then at me. Her mouth was wide open, and her eyes were even wider. Now I had to ask her the question. "Did you hear it too?"

"*Rachel Kowalski...recording?* Yes I heard that—loud and clear. Who was that, Rachel? One of your little cousins?" The more she spoke, the more agitated she became. "Did you record over something else? What's going on? Tell me the truth—I have to know!"

"I don't think I should. I mean, Ashland asked me not to be all spooky with you, but I swear I'm not making this up. I mean, you heard it yourself! Before you arrived, I went up to the attic to do some recon, and I did some video documentation myself. You know, to get the feel of the place." I took a deep breath. "And I heard a voice. It mocked me, like an echo. I think it was a child's voice. That's what you heard. Somehow I managed to record it. But that's not the weird part."

She swallowed visibly. "It's not?"

"No. What's weird is the recording is from another card. This new recording, the one with your second take, is on a new card. An entirely brand new card. I hadn't even opened this card until after I left the attic. There's no way that the voice recorded onto a card that wasn't in the camera. I can't explain it. I'm sorry, Carrie Jo. I know I sound—well..."

"No apologies necessary, but let's try to keep it together. Okay? Maybe the camera has some built-in storage. Some of them do. It's possible that you think you recorded on the card but you actually recorded on the camera's storage drive. That is a possibility, right?"

"I guess so."

"Let's go with that for now. And Ashland had no right to ask you to do that. I'm not afraid of the supernatural, Rachel. He is. You can always talk to me, but until we know for sure what's going on, let's keep it between us. And for goodness' sake, don't mention it to the client. Since the goal here is to make this a place he can rent for weddings, balls and the like, I'm sure he wouldn't like this too much. He's not the kind of guy to condone any talk about ghosts and such."

"You're probably right." I took the card out of the camera. "Now what do I do with these creepy things?"

"If you wouldn't mind, I can ask Henri to take a listen. He's hip with the supernatural media stuff. I dream about it, Ashland sees it, but Henri is real good at cataloging it."

"What's Detra Ann's superpower, then?" I smiled at Carrie Jo, hoping she'd ask me about mine.

"She's our lie detector. She knows when someone is lying. It's pretty cool to watch her."

"That just leaves me. I guess I'm the only one in our group who doesn't have a superpower." It felt good to be considered a part of the gang.

She patted my shoulder and said, "That's not true at all. You do too have a superpower. You are a *sensitive*, Rachel. You can sense things, and apparently record them. In my book, that's way better because you've got some real proof, if that's what this is."

As she spoke, I believed her. No lie detector needed. CJ didn't have a lying bone in her body. Then I got the distinct feeling that someone was watching us, and I quickly saw that I was right. A burly young man was peering in the window next to the front door of Idlewood.

"Hang on, I've got this." I handed her the camera so she could look at it. I hoped against hope that I hadn't damaged it in any way. I wasn't careful enough with my own equipment. Imagine throwing it down like that. I could have damaged the evidence.

I opened the door and smiled. "May I help you?"

"Are you Carrie Jo Stuart?"

"No, but I'm her assistant. I'm Rachel. Who might you be?"

"Oh, sorry." He extended his hand, and I shook it like I was meeting a church date, although he didn't give me the church date vibe. "My name is Angus. I'm an electrician, and my specialty is bringing these grand old homes up to date. Quite nice to see that someone is willing to restore Idlewood. Very exciting."

"You're Scottish, Angus?"

"What gave it away? My accent, my beard or my name?"

To my own surprise I said, "I wish I could say it was your kilt, but since you aren't wearing one, I'll have to say your beard. No, wait. The name. The name and the accent." He laughed heartily at that. I liked this red-haired giant of a man already. He was probably my age, maybe a year or two older. While he ran his fingers through his wavy red hair, I took a peek at his hands. Nope. No ring.

Geesh, it's not like me to flirt quite so obviously, but hey, this is fun. It had been a long time since anyone had turned my head, but I had to stay professional. "I'm just babbling. Sorry. Follow me, please, Angus. Meet the boss lady. Carrie Jo, this is Angus. He's the electrician here to work his magic."

"Wonderful! What's the problem, Angus?"

He sputtered at first but then began to explain how certain breakers had to be replaced, that the wiring was old and some of the lines were beyond burnt. He would like to begin immediately and felt sure he could get it straightened out today. "Can't leave such lovely Southern ladies to freeze to death. It's going to get chilly this afternoon."

"That settles it, then. We can finish our documentation later. We need that electricity to get our computers set up. This is a big day for us, Angus," I spoke up. Carrie Jo was looking more tired by the minute.

"Good. Excuse me a minute. I'll go get my tools."

I watched him walk out of the house and smiled at Carrie Jo. "Hubba, hubba, CJ. What do you think?"

"Oh, he's not my type. My type is a blue-eyed, blond football player with shoulders that sway when he walks…and I've been such a jerk to him today." She plopped down in the chair and scanned through her phone. I had an idea.

"Go home, boss lady. Leave your son at day care and go home. Go take a nap, go get your hair done. Do something just for you, Carrie Jo. You deserve it."

At that, she smiled weakly. "Seriously? I can't do that. I have to work."

"What work? We can't do anything right now. We have no electricity. And if Angus is going to do all he plans to do, it might be hours or days before it's on." I didn't really have any idea how long it would take, but it was true that we probably wouldn't do anything else today. Thankfully Angus wasn't here to contradict me.

"I am tired. It's true. Would you mind? Are you going to be safe here with a couple of strange guys?"

"I'm sure I will. I think I can handle myself."

"All right. I swear I'll have my head in the game tomorrow. I'll be here early."

I hugged her. "It's no big deal, CJ. If for some reason the Taylors stop by, I'll make your excuses." I looked around at the peeling wallpaper, the dirty floors, the broken and missing crown molding. "From the way things are going here, it looks like you and I are both going to need some naps."

She grabbed her keys, purse and briefcase and left without much more arguing. I sat down at the desk waiting for Angus to return. After about fifteen minutes, he hadn't, so I walked outside to see what the holdup was.

There was no truck. There was no Angus. I couldn't even see where there had been tire tracks in the driveway except for mine and Carrie Jo's. *What the heck?* I walked around the property through the wild stickers I'd vowed to avoid earlier, ripping my skin a few times. I couldn't make it all the way to the back of the house, so I circled back to the front and went the other way. There wasn't much out there, just vine-covered buildings: what looked like it used to be a greenhouse, the corner of a brick platform and some other bumps in the landscape. It was a forbidding place. And suddenly I felt very alone. I called out to Angus a few times, but I spotted neither him nor his truck.

What if he wasn't really an electrician but someone from the neighborhood looking to rob me or rip off some of the few valuable pieces left at Idlewood? That just didn't make sense. Why would he show up wearing work overalls? And why would he introduce himself to us? I walked back inside and called out a few more times. I quietly grabbed my stuff, closed the door behind me, locked it up tight and left the house.

That was enough for one day. More than enough. I didn't linger. I didn't wait for anyone else to show up. I drove down the driveway and sat at the end of the street trying to decide where I should go next. Home to show the video to Mom and Gran, then call my aunts? They would all definitely be interested, but then Mom and Gran would want to come visit the house, and I didn't think CJ would go for that. Not with the owners being so close-minded about spiritual activity and all. No, I needed to take it to Henri myself. CJ had left the video card here, and I wanted to hear firsthand what he had to say.

But what could he say? *Yep, that's a ghost you have there.*

As I sat in my car I could almost hear the voice again. The small, young voice of someone who wanted my attention. Someone who wasn't alive, most likely.

Rachel Kowalski…recording…

I headed down Dauphin to Cotton City Treasures, his antiques store. I hoped Henri was in Mobile and not taking one of his many trips to New Orleans.

I needed answers—and pretty darn quick!

Chapter Three—Henri

I'd barely gotten my first cup of coffee down when the first customer of the day walked into the shop. She was a window-shopper who didn't make a purchase, but I helped her and she left with a few flyers for the upcoming Dauphin Street Fair that we would be participating in. I sat behind the counter again and worked on my new website design for Haunted Gulf Coast. It was more of a hobby, something to fuel my lifelong obsession with the supernatural. Thanks to some of Detra Ann's string-pulling, I'd managed to get permission to spend one night at Lee House near the old courthouse. The owners were big believers in spiritual things, and they claimed this particular spot was full of negative energy. I told them I couldn't help at all with "cleansing the place" but I would be more than happy to investigate. Maybe I could capture something. I was looking forward to the adventure. It had been a while since I'd done anything like it, although I had a sneaking suspicion that I'd be going solo. My better half was more practical than I was, although she had her own set of abilities that surprised even me sometimes.

Detra Ann and our one and only employee, Aimee, had gone to the Big Buy, as they liked to call it. It was a monthly regional auction for antiques dealers. The last time they made the trip across the bay, they came back with a truck full of real treasures. I hoped they were as lucky this time because business was booming. Really booming, thanks to the recent surge in old home restorations in the area. We had Seven Sisters to thank for that. Detra Ann knew the story behind each piece acquired, and Aimee was great at getting the prices we wanted.

When I wasn't tracking down local ghosts, I was spending all my free time looking through old newspaper clippings about Aleezabeth. I'd been on the phone with Dumont's new sheriff, Harry Joseph, but just like before, I wasn't getting anywhere. Local law enforcement didn't seem to care. Aleezabeth had disappeared so long ago that the case was technically "cold" and not given the priority it deserved. At least that was what I suspected. I didn't want to believe it was because we had dark skin, or because we came from a poor family, but how else would you explain it? How could someone just disappear into thin air and nobody know anything or seem to care that a sweet young person who wouldn't harm a fly had vanished?

To tell the truth, I felt a little let down. I'd hoped Carrie Jo and Ashland would help me find my cousin after everything settled down in their own lives, but that didn't happen. To be fair, I'd kind of put it out of my mind too. Until Lenore began turning up in my bedroom, my car, the store. She never spoke and wouldn't look at me. Her presence was enough. She was ashamed of my lack of purpose. My failure to get to the bottom of the mystery. I heard her whisper once: *No more Peas, Carrots and Onions.* Only I was left, and I wasn't doing too well with my investigation into the disappearance of my own cousin. And I had two deaths to answer for now. I felt I didn't deserve to be happy. I think Lenore agreed. Not when she and Aleezabeth were gone and apparently forgotten.

And here I was, about to marry the woman of my dreams like nothing had ever happened. My grandmother died shortly after Aleezabeth's disappearance, but I was pretty sure she'd think it was shameful. I was the man in the family, after all, and now I was the only family left. Aleezabeth had been my responsibility. I'd let her down.

"Come on, Harry. It's not your fault," Detra Ann would tell me. Only she could call me Harry and get away with it. I'd pretend I agreed with her, but I didn't. Not at all. Every detail of that day was ingrained in my head. I had been so anxious to do my own thing, to get into my own mischief, that I could not be bothered with my cousin. And I had left her alone. Alone to be grabbed by some evil man who stole her away from us all. No. I couldn't tell Detra Ann all this. I internalized it and continued to search. Sometimes she'd help me sort through copies of stolen police reports. (Thankfully she didn't ask questions about where I got them; she just raised her perfectly arched blond eyebrow and continued to read.) Yes, I loved this woman.

She'd taken a lot of heat after we announced our engagement, but she handled everything with grace. We were just talking about our engagement party this morning. It was a few months ago, but since her mother was such a socialite the Old Mobile crowd continued to whisper about us. Detra Ann laughed with me remembering Jessica Cumbest's reaction to our big news. She'd swanned over for a personal chat at our engagement reception.

"Detra Ann, *I* don't have a problem with you marrying someone *like* Henri. I just hope you understand some folks will—have a problem, I mean. There are some differences that are just too much for people to overlook."

My fiancée sweetly replied in a whisper that matched Jessica's, "Henri and I have talked about this quite a bit. We both feel like we can handle the age difference pretty well. I mean, he's only ten years older than me. It's not like he's twenty years my senior." Jessica's face had turned red, and we sailed away to greet the rest of our "friends." That was another reason to love Detra Ann, and as if she knew I was thinking about her she sent me a text.

I got the Steenburg! I got the Steenburg!

That had been her big goal today. Find a cast-iron Steenburg statue for Mrs. Devries, one of our most faithful customers. Mrs. Devries reminded me of someone I used to know, but I couldn't quite put my finger on it. It would come to me eventually.

I continued clicking around on the page, rearranging components. I'd just about gotten the site like I wanted it when I felt a subtle moving of the air and caught a whiff of Lenore's favorite perfume. It was the same kind our grandmother wore on special occasions, something called Vanderbilt. Then as if she were standing next to me I heard Lenore say, *"Can't you at least say her name, Henri?"*

"It's Aleezabeth! Aleezabeth! All right?" I said to the empty room. That was the moment Rachel came busting in the shop looking like she had run all the way here.

"Oh good. You're here." She looked around the shop and, seeing no one else, talked a mile a minute. "I've got something to show you—no. I've got something you should listen to. I captured it on my camera this morning. It's from Idlewood." She slid off her black jacket and tossed it across the glass counter, then tugged up the long sleeves of her gray t-shirt. Rachel knew all about my hobby documenting supernatural events, but I never expected her to share anything with me. She'd been courteous about the subject but not so much that I would have ever imagined she'd want me to collaborate with her. Not about Idlewood. Her Katie Holmes bob hairstyle bounced around her young face as she talked animatedly with her hands. Yep, she looked so much like the actress that sometimes I had to look twice. But she was just Rachel or Rachel K, as she called herself. Bubbly kid sister to our group of friends.

"Call me curious. What do you have?"

"It's on my digital storage card. Actually, I have two. Can you take a look at them with me?"

"I've got the laptop right here. Hand me the card, and we'll load it onto the big monitor over there."

"For the record, this is all legit. CJ told me to bring this over to you. But the owner of the house, Desmond Taylor, well, he shouldn't know about it. He's kind of funny about these things." She pulled one card out of the camera and one from her jeans pocket and handed them to me.

"Not a problem. Let's see what you got."

While we waited for the program to open, she shuffled through my stack of papers, as always without asking permission. "Still nothing, huh? I meant to ask you if you'd heard anything about your cousin. Maybe we should all load up and go over to Dumont. I bet with everyone's help we could figure out what happened to her. Or at least help you find some clues as to where to look next." She put the papers back and leaned forward with her hands on her knees. "This is it. Just forward about twenty seconds and then— yes! There! Turn up the volume!"

I did as she asked me and almost fell out of my chair when I heard the voice whispering Rachel's name. "What the..." I slid the player tab back and listened again. "Okay, set it up for me. What was happening when you got this audio?"

She told me the whole story, and I felt the gooseflesh rise on my arms. "Let's look at the whole thing this time. Let me start it over." I listened to Rachel's chatty voice on the recording and studied the room as she panned around and pointed at different focal points. "There!" I shouted. "Did you see it? It's a shadow."

"What?" she said, moving closer to the screen.

"Look just there, under the small window at the end of the building. There's an empty space there, but in a second you'll see a shadow fall across the wall and then disappear." I pointed to the place where I wanted her to look, skipped the video back and played it again. There it was. A small shadow moving quickly across the faded white wall. "And you didn't see anything while you were there?"

"Not a thing. I can't believe I'm seeing it now!" she said, pushing her long bangs out of her eyes. She stared at the screen as if she still couldn't believe what she was seeing. "It's so small and the voice...so young...it must be a child. Do you think I caught something real?"

"Or it wants you to think it is a child. That would definitely make it more sympathetic. But it sounds real enough to me, and of course it is possible that it is the real deal." She chewed on her lip and gave me a fearful look. When she was finished mulling it over we watched it again, this time with the sound muted.

"That's so creepy. Every time I watch, it just gets creepier."

I sensed there was something else about this experience that she hadn't told me yet. "Anything else?"

"Well, I'm not sure if this is paranormal or not, but it sure was weird. There was this guy, a young guy with red hair and a beard. He showed up, said his name was Angus. He was supposed to be working on the electrical in the house, but he disappeared. I mean, not like vanished before my eyes, but he went out to his truck to get his tools and never came back."

"Truck disappeared too?"

"No, I never actually saw the truck. He just said he had one. And he was Scottish. Did you know the first two families in that house were Scottish?"

"That's pretty weak grounds for calling him a ghost, Rach. Aren't there Scottish folks in Alabama?" I couldn't help but laugh.

She punched my arm and said, "Come on, really? How many do you know? Name one and I'll believe you. I think he *was* a ghost."

"I'm not ready to make that call yet, but I wasn't there. We'd have to see if he shows up again. He might just be a very alive, very human ne'er-do-well looking to get into mischief. And I know for a fact Mobile has plenty of those."

"Yeah, true enough. I hope he wasn't one. Before I thought he was a ghost or a ne'er-do-well, I thought he was cute. I'd hate to think he was dead." A red flush spread across her cheeks and nose. "And he seemed so human, so alive. No. You're right. There has to be another explanation."

I shrugged. "Maybe there is. Maybe he was a guardian spirit coming to check on the house. That has happened before.

He might have thought you were cute too." I chuckled at her. "But let me see what we can find out." I typed in Idle-wood in my site's search feature. There were no hits for that house on Haunted Gulf Coast, which only meant nobody had made a report about the place. I went wide and typed the name and the city into the Haunted Web's search engine. It was basically a search engine that plundered all things paranormal. It was a huge net that caught much more than I could with my wimpy little website. "Hey, look at this."

"I just spent three months researching the house's history, and I didn't see anything like this. How did I miss all these reports?" she asked incredulously.

"You historians. If you ever want to research hauntings, you have to skip the educational websites. Science doesn't like this kind of stuff. This is the search engine to use when you're ghost hunting. There are at least fifteen mentions of Idlewood, and that was with a general search."

"Well, click on some," she said impatiently.

With a shake of my head I clicked the first item. I knew immediately we had a winner. The headline read: IDLE-WOOD'S FORGOTTEN CHILDREN.

"Shoot!" Rachel dug her phone out of her purse as it chimed away. "Oh no. This is Mr. Taylor. I'd better take it. He's probably wondering where we are." She answered the phone and stepped outside for some privacy. I nodded absently and quickly scanned through the article. After plowing through stacks of papers, emails and websites recently, I'd gotten good at scanning through documents and pulling out the important details. I read aloud the part that seemed most significant.

"Idlewood Plantation in Mobile, Alabama, has many secrets—including the location of two of the five Ferguson children who disappeared on or around the property in the 1870s following the death of their oldest sister, fifteen-year-old Tallulah Ferguson. The house has been closed to the public for many years, but older reports suggest the spirits of the 'lost children' manifest as shadowy figures in certain parts of the house..."

The bell on the door rang loudly as Rachel walked back inside. She held the phone to her chin and pressed her back against the door. "I have to go," she said slowly. She seemed extremely distracted.

"You want me to email you this list?"

"Yeah, that would be great." She pulled on her coat and grabbed her purse.

"Everything okay, Rachel?"

"That was indeed Mr. Taylor, wondering why we weren't at the house. What a jerk! I told him we weren't there because the power wasn't on, and he didn't believe me. He said he knew it was on because he just left there. He says it's been on all week. Can you believe that? I checked it myself, Henri. Nothing was working. I'd better go back. I hate to call Carrie Jo—she's not, um, feeling too well, and she'd flip out if she knew she missed Mr. Taylor. He didn't sound too happy. I'd better get back there."

"Hey! Don't forget your cards."

"No, you keep them for now. I've really got to go. Don't forget to send me those links, please. Thanks for everything."

"No problem. Thanks for sharing them. And hey, I might take you up on that Dumont trip. I might need some help." She nodded with a sweet smile, and I watched her leave. Then I went back to the video and turned the volume back up.

I flicked the video back and watched the small shadow slide across the wall just as before. I saw Rachel's finger pointing to different focal points in the room. Now came the part I wanted to analyze with my software. I grabbed a pen and a piece of paper and waited to write down the time marker on the video. I expected to hear a child's voice speak again, but it wasn't a child's voice that I heard now.

It was a man—no doubt it was a man's voice. The voice sounded darker and more menacing than any I could remember. And it didn't say, "Rachel Kowalski...recording."

It very clearly said, "*Stay away!*"

Chapter Four—Carrie Jo

I drove home in a fog—a brain fog. My mind felt sticky, and a sudden onset of the yawns hit me hard. Never had I wanted a nap more than right now. The lack of electricity at Idlewood had really been a blessing in disguise for this new mommy, because I don't think I could have made it through the day without some shut-eye. I glanced at my watch. Yep, I had three glorious hours of uninterrupted sleep.

In five minutes I was in my driveway. Lately, Ashland and I had gotten in the habit of pulling our cars into the back-yard. There'd been a rash of car radio robberies a few months ago, and although we hadn't been hit, a few of our neighbors had. I loved living in historic downtown Mobile, but it did have a downside—the occasional outburst of crime. I hoped the city got it under control soon. Many of us were on edge, including me, but I was mostly just so darned tired. I pressed the button on the remote, pulled the car past the gate, closed it behind me and walked back up the sidewalk to my front door. I could have entered through the back door, but I locked the dead bolt when I left this morning. At least I thought I had. Dang. My brain was *ti-red*.

Unfortunately, my new neighbor, Mrs. Astrid Peterson, spotted me as I pulled in and was headed my way, her water hose in her gloved hand. She and my mother had become friends during Momma's stay, but Mrs. Peterson was too much of a busybody for my taste. In my experience if someone was willing to gossip about your friends or neighbors, they would be willing to gossip about you too. Before I rounded the corner of my Victorian home, I dug my phone out of my purse. And like a big fat liar, I pretended to get a call and slapped the phone to my ear as I walked to the door, juggling my keys in my hand. With a cheery, awkward wave, I stepped inside and closed the door behind me.

Never had I been so happy to be safely inside Our Little Home. I locked the door and debated climbing the stairs to my bedroom. Nah, I'd just hit the hay in the downstairs guestroom. For all of thirty seconds, I mulled over calling Ashland. I wasn't above eating some crow—I'd been snacking on it quite a bit lately—but I put it off until after my nap. I tossed my purse and keys on the dresser and kicked off my shoes. With sleepy eyes I set the alarm on my phone and pulled back the fluffy white comforter. It looked like a heavenly cloud, and I fell into it quickly. I was asleep in no time.

I slept so peacefully that I woke up only once, worried that I'd missed the alarm. I hadn't. I had another hour. One more hour of restorative sleep. I cuddled back up with the comforter, still tired but thinking of all the things I'd intended to do today at Idlewood.

Idlewood was such a lovely old home.

I could almost see it as it had been, although there were no oil paintings of the home from that time period.

It was so lovely that I could practically imagine newly planted crepe myrtles in the front yard, blue hydrangeas filling up the flowerbeds around the porches. I could see the white curtains blowing in a cool spring breeze. The blue sky above, the grass freshly mowed with scythes, the hounds played with a little girl.

Yes, there was a little girl. A girl with large, expressive hazel eyes. And they had seen too much, too soon. She had streaks of pink on her cheeks, pink from playing with the dogs. Her long light brown hair was curled in ringlets that freely fell across her narrow shoulders. She wore an overly large pink bow in her hair, which made her look even younger since she was small for her age. Her name was Trinket…

***

Sister? Are you there? I can feel you with me. I listened but heard nothing, no whisper of acknowledgement. I must be imagining things. I like to imagine so many things.

I giggled as the dog tugged at the stick in my hand, and I finally freed it from the hound's slobbering mouth. Feeling suddenly guilty for laughing, I tossed the stick away, and the brown and white spotted hound chased after it. I had no thought that moment beyond the desire to play forever until I heard *his* voice. And then my heart filled with fear, like a well fills up with cold water whenever one draws from it. It was the deep-down-in-your-bones kind of cold that stole all the joy from your soul. Yes, he was a joy-stealer.

And he was my brother.

"Coming, Michael," I answered him dutifully. He was the man of the house now. Father was dead, and Mother had stopped speaking altogether and pretended that we were *all* dead. Not just my sister. Percy left Idlewood again and left weeping Aubrey behind. She'd mostly kept to her room until he returned because she believed there was a ghost in the house. I was partly responsible for her belief.

So in fact, there were only the three of us now: Michael, Bridget the Queen of the Fairies, as she commanded us all to call her, and me. I walked through the field of flowers to the house, rubbing my hands across the blooms, across the sea of purple blooms as I went along quietly. It was almost as if I were swimming in flowers. I wished I could swim away forever. There was no love in this house.

I reminded myself it was time to be an adult. Michael would expect it. And when he left again, I would be a child once more. Me against the Queen of the Fairies, for all the others were gone.

And how I miss Tallulah! I am told not to speak her name or think of her. She is forever separated from us—she is in purgatory for all eternity. That's what they say, but I have seen her. How do they explain that? Yes, she committed a mortal sin, yet I could not stop weeping for her in secret because I knew she had never left us, and yet I must shun her. Yes, we were told to never speak her name, but the desire to do so is there—on the tip of my tongue. Just once I want to say it aloud. Just once, in honor of the girl who had been so lovely and kind and just a little mad. But she'd always been mad in a dear, sweet way, and we all wanted to protect her, love her. Even Bridget. I wanted to scream her name, for I loved her. I forgave her, so why couldn't God? Sometimes I imagined myself climbing to the tip-top of the roof of Idlewood. Yes, even now I could see myself standing there, and there I would victoriously blast a scream…

"Tallulah! I miss you, Tallulah Ferguson!"

But it was only a dream, only a wish. For if I were to do it and the priest was correct, then I am sure God would strike me dead. The priest said, "She is lost forever. Do not speak her name or you shall bring damnation upon yourself, child."

And I know someday I shall indeed say her name. She will not be forgotten. Not forever!

"I am coming, Michael. I am on the way!"

***

My alarm blared annoyingly, and as I reached for my phone, the sweet essence of Trinket's spirit slipped away from me, evacuating my dream like a tiny cloud. What a strange experience. But it made me doubly glad that I was now working at Idlewood, a place where this loving yet fearful child lived some time ago. How sad to witness the pain of the broken family. I pulled the covers back and stretched but froze as I put my shoes on.

Oh my God! Someone was in my house! Was it Doreen? No, I could hear a man speaking in low tones—and there was a woman too. Hey! Was that Ashland? I wanted to run out of the room and put my arms around him, tell him all about my dream, but something told me to hold back. And I could hear them arguing about something. This seemed so strange.

I leaned against the bedroom wall, inched toward the door and listened like a nosy detective. If they were arguing, I wanted to know about it. I hoped it wasn't about me. Libby Stevenson often put her nose where it didn't belong. But I didn't hear anything else. It was strangely quiet. I slid my shoes off again and walked quietly toward the sound of their voices. I turned the corner, and there was Ashland. He had his back to me, and Libby's arms were around his neck. They were kissing! Before I could say, "You sonofabitch!" he'd pushed her away and said, "Whoa! What's the deal, Libby?"

He just thought I was fuming earlier. I was highly ticked now. So ticked in fact that I shot across the room and let her know what I thought of her. "You've got a lot of damn nerve kissing my husband! Get out of my house, Libby, before I beat your ass!"

To my surprise she smiled at me coyly. "Now, Carrie Jo, I know you haven't been feeling well lately. I don't know what you think you saw, but we weren't doing anything wrong. Tell her, Ashland."

Ashland backed away from her and came to stand by me, and together we glared at her. "I don't know what kind of game you're playing, but I'm not part of it. Now get out, Libby. Our working relationship is hereby terminated."

She looked shocked but didn't make a move to leave our home. "No. I don't think we're done yet. You can't deny what we have, Ash, baby. It's time to make a decision. It's her or me. You can't have your cake and eat it too." She hovered in front of him seductively, just a foot away. I couldn't believe what I was seeing. She batted her big cow eyes at him.

"You better call the police, Ashland, because it's about to go down in here." I started taking off my jewelry. I had never been in a fight in my entire life, but I'd seen this in a movie once. Stripping off jewelry meant you were ready to throw down, I think. I took out my pearl posts. Took off my wedding band and started on my watch. Libby didn't wait for me to get my watch off. She threw herself at me like a high-heeled banshee, scratching at me with her manicured nails.

"What is your problem? Can't find your own man?" I taunted her. "You are pitiful Libby!" I slapped across her face, leaving a nice red mark on her cheek. She raised a fist and punched me in my mouth. I tasted the blood but didn't feel any pain. All I saw was red! I couldn't believe how quickly my day was evolving. For some reason I laughed, and she looked at me like I was crazy.

"You think that's bad? That's the best you got? I just gave birth to an eight-pound baby! Is that it?" I have no idea where the smack talk came from, but I had it in abundance at the moment. I guess my nap had made me cocky.

Ash stepped in between us, but that was the wrong thing to do. "Stop that, Carrie Jo. Last chance for you to leave, Libby." We were like two wild cats scratching and clawing at one another. Unfortunately, one of her freakish punches landed square on my jaw and sent me tumbling on top of the coffee table. I gasped as I hit the ground, smacking my temple hard on the table and then the wooden floor. The last thing I remembered was, "Darn, that was a lucky shot."

Then everything melted away. I was no longer in Our Little Home. My husband, my son and Libby had vanished like smoke. For a second or two I didn't know where I was, and I squinted against the light. It shone first like a pinpoint in a fabric of darkness and quickly expanded and became a bright sunny day.

If I hadn't recognized the rounded ceiling with the painted wooden panels, the stacked gold fireplace sconces that I ordered replicas for and the view from the long row of windows, I would never have known that I was at Idlewood.

Chapter Five—Trinket

"The world belongs to Percy and Tallulah. They are the Golden Children, Trinket. Why do you bother to tempt Mother to speak to us? Do you think Mother cares or even sees us now that her favorite daughter killed herself?" I frowned at Bridget for those cruel words, but little did I know or understand how true they really were.

Percy and Tallulah had indeed been the "Golden Ones," as we called them. My older sister and brother, twins, had golden hair, sparkling light eyes and perfect faces. And they were tall and slender like the elegant fairies in Bridget's books—images that she practically worshiped. How she hated her own dark looks! I wanted to point out to her that Mother was neither perfect nor golden, but it would do me little good, and she was so distraught now that the point seemed moot. Percy and Tallulah had loved us, of that I had no doubt, but they kept the greatest part of their love for one another. When Tallulah was alive and we were all young and happy, they were rarely separated until Father told Percy it was time for him to marry. Percy and Father argued extensively on the subject, but Father was resolute in his commandment. For the "Golden Ones" there would be no more long walks together by themselves. No more riding around the countryside—Percy on Ol' Blackie and Tallulah on the dappled gray she called Dumpling. They were cast out of their secret world, and Mother was power-less to intervene as she always had before. Something had happened that I did not understand. In the end I supposed they'd merely crossed the invisible silver line and entered adulthood, a land where there was no fun, only duty and unhappiness.

To gather more information, I attempted to spy on the household, for there was always plenty of gossip. We had many servants who liked to talk about the people they served. As I always did when I wanted to know something that I wasn't supposed to hear, I'd climb in the dumbwaiter, the wooden box on a rope that the servants used sometimes to haul laundry and dishes up and down. I'd hitch the rope around my hand and lower myself down to the servants' quarters or pull with all my might and take the box to the second floor. More than once I'd been discovered, for the dumbwaiter was a noisy thing.

Mrs. Potts would try to box my ears, but I always escaped her grasp. I don't think she really tried to punish me, although she'd boxed Michael's ears more than once when he stole food from the pantry or played with her matches.

Yes, Percy and Tallulah had been the Golden Ones, and the rest of us, Bridget, Michael and I, were not as beautiful or as intelligent. Or as special.

Bridget had dark brown hair with dark eyes like Michael's, but I was the changeling, as my only living sister liked to call me. According to her taunts, and she was one to be cruel, the real Trinket Ferguson had been stolen from the crib and I, a product of evil fairies, was the child they chose to leave behind. I was a changeling, she said. "Probably belonged to some gypsy mother." Her words no longer made me cry. I knew them for what they were, her own pain projected onto others. Bridget, the family actress, worked very hard to hide her feelings from anyone who might care. She didn't want us to know she cared about anything at all, except her fairies, which she looked for day and night. She'd even taken to making them furniture and clothing from bits of leftover dress scraps. I helped her once in a while when she was in a mood for company. Most of the time she was not. She preferred her books and her tiny companions, which I could never see. I wanted to see them for Bridget's sake, but no matter how hard I searched I never found one. And I wasn't sure Bridget actually saw them either.

No, of my two sisters, Tallulah had been the kinder one. But it had not always been so. I remember when Bridget kissed me goodnight and said prayers with me. That stopped one night, and it was as if my sister left and she was the changeling. If it had not been for Tallulah, I would have had no kisses goodnight and no bedtime stories. She had been a gentle spirit with faraway eyes and a sweet voice that always sounded as if she were out of breath. How she enchanted us all!

Just before her death, the announcement was made that Tallulah had been promised to Richard Chestnut, a respectable young man from Conecuh County, whatever that meant. I supposed "respectable" meant people respected him, but who knew, really? I didn't think much of him at all.

Tallulah met him only once when he came with his father to sign the legal documents. I hated him instantly. He licked his lips a lot at my sister like he was a cat and she a tiny bird-lunch. A shame, too, because he wasn't old or ugly or poor. Repulsed, Tallulah kept her eyes averted for the rest of the meeting and stood shaking at Father's side during their formal introductions. So disturbed was I by his behavior that I went to both Mother and Father and made my plea on Tallulah's behalf. If she wouldn't object, I would do it for her. I described Richard Chestnut's unpleasant demeanor in great detail to my mother, who declared there were much worse things to be offended by. My father listened patiently for less than a minute and then dismissed me as a nosy child. I went seeking Tallulah to tell her how sorry I was and how I'd tried to help, but it took a while to find her. She was nowhere in the house, not even in the dumbwaiter. Bridget wouldn't help me look, as she was headed to the pond with a new set of fairy furniture she'd stolen from my dollhouse. Feeling aggravated, more about her lack of concern for Tallulah than about the furniture, I stomped my foot to display my disapproval and continued with my search.

She was in the Great Oak behind the house. The one with the very long, wide branch that two people could lie on. Sometimes, when Percy wasn't around, she let me lie beside her, and we'd watch the squirrels scamper across the branches above us. They sent showers of leaves down upon us, and we'd laugh and laugh. That was where I found her that unfortunate day. Only she wasn't watching the squirrels. She was straddling the branch and had an oily-looking rope in her hands. I didn't put two and two together at that moment, but I did as I heard the determination in her voice. Tallulah tied the end of the rope to the tree with a shoelace knot. Just the idea that my sister would consider such a thing offended me greatly. I'd never seen an actual hanging, but Bridget drew me an awful picture one time of a hanged man. Hanged for stealing a horse. He had a blue face and he had wet his pants. It made me gag and cry.

"What are you doing, Lula?" I called up to her as she fiddled with the noose. She didn't answer me, and it was then that I noticed she was quietly crying and talking to herself. No, praying. That disturbed me even more.

"Please, please, Lula. Answer me!"

She paused and stared at me from behind a curtain of blond hair that covered part of her face. "Run away, Trinket! I don't want you to see me like this. I can't let you see me die."

"Noooo! You can't leave me, Tallulah! I would die too, and so would Percy!"

"Percy is here?" she asked, wiping her face with the back of her hand. She leaned forward and stared in the direction of the house. I wanted to tell her yes just to get her down from the tree, but I could not bring myself to deceive her. She'd been mistreated enough for one day.

"No, but it is almost time for the mail to come, Lula. What would happen if Percy's letter came and you weren't there to collect it? I heard Bridget say she would read the next one." Well, that *was* a lie. Bridget did not care two flying figs about letters from Percy, but my sisters were famous for squabbling over everything. Why not this? And if it distracted Tallulah, surely God would approve.

She started crying again, and I felt even more concerned. What should I do? How could I save her? Then I had a brilliant idea. Or at least I thought it was brilliant. "You can't die, Tallulah. I asked Bridget to cast a fairy spell on you. You will live forever now. You'll just have to hang yourself and then dangle from the rope until someone finds you."

"You know there are no such things as fairies, much less fairy spells. Please go now, Trinket, so I can end my miserable life!"

"What if I'm not lying? What if she did cast a spell on you? And what if Percy's letter is already at the house? Please come down. Things will change. You'll see. You can't give up, Tallulah."

She slid the poorly tied noose around her neck, leaned forward against the tree branch and hugged it like it was her only friend. "I'm going to do it, Trinket. I am going to cast myself down from here and snap my neck. I want to die!" She let a panicked sob escape her lips. I wanted to sob with her, but that would solve nothing. I let her continue. Perhaps she merely needed someone to talk to. "I cannot marry that boy. He is disgusting. You saw him! I can't!" She sobbed and cried, and I sat in the scant grass below the tree. "Why did he leave me here, Trinket?"

I knew it was Percy she referred to. I sighed and said, "To obey Father, I suppose. But he won't be gone forever, Lula. He won't be! In fact, he'll be home in two weeks. That's what Mrs. Potts told the miller when he stopped by this morning. Just two weeks! How sad he'll be to know you died while he was gone. I think you will break his heart, Tallulah. And who loves you more than anyone in the world?"

"Percy?" she whispered hopefully. "It's Percy. But I love you too, Trinket. Never think that I don't. It's just different for us because we're—well, we are…"

"I know, I know. You are twins. I understand, Tallulah." I tried to sound like the admission didn't hurt me, like I was as mature as my fifteen-year-old sister. We sat for a while, and she didn't come down, but I could tell she was thinking about it. She'd quit crying, and we heard someone calling us in the distance. "You know, if anyone could make him come home earlier, it would be you."

She took the noose off her neck and rubbed her pale skin. The rough rope had reddened it. "What do you mean?"

"You should write him. Tell him what happened today and ask him to talk to Father for you. If anyone can help you, it would certainly be Percy. I tried to speak for you, but no one listens to me." I folded my arms across my chest and felt sullen. She started climbing down the tree, her blue dress threatening to trip her. I was happy to see that she'd left the rope up on the branch. Later I would come and steal it away so she didn't change her mind and sneak back here when I wasn't about.

"I listen to you," she said as she sat down beside me, holding out her arms.

I flew into them and put my arms around her neck. Now that she was down and safe, I cried on her already red neck. "Please don't leave me, Tallulah."

"Shush now. I am here, see? I won't leave yet. I am going to write to Percy and tell him Father's horrible plan. He will come home and stop him, I know he will. Everything will be as it once was, dearest. Shush now." Tallulah held me for a few more minutes, but eventually we would have to heed the call from the house. Together we rose from the grass and walked toward Idlewood. I held her hand, refusing to let it go, as if she would run back at any moment and throw herself from the tree. At least I stopped her that day. How was I supposed to know she would try again? I should have told someone. I should have told Mother about the rope. I should have asked Bridget for the fairy spell I threatened Tallulah with.

I did none of those things, and now Tallulah was dead. Even worse, she would always be forgotten, her name never to be uttered in public or in private. And the banishment would force her lovely face from our memories forever.

And it was all my fault.

Chapter Six—Rachel

I walked into Idlewood with a polite smile and offered the man waiting for me a handshake. "Hi, Mr. Taylor. I'm Rachel. We have met before, at the Stuarts' office when you came in to sign the paperwork for the house? I am sorry Carrie Jo isn't with me. She's off acquiring something for your house, no doubt. When we were here this morning, there was no electricity at all."

"Yes, I remember you." Desmond Taylor was not the kind of guy who wasted time on pleasantries and such. Not that he was necessarily rude. I think the word I was looking for was "professional." Extremely professional. He'd insisted that someone come to the house, probably because he wanted to let us know he wasn't happy that we hadn't come out of the box like gangbusters. Unlike Ashland, who enjoyed the slow, steady process of the restoration, Mr. Taylor was all about the bottom line. The sooner we could get this place ready for use in his wife's party planning business, the better. I could just about read the man; he reminded me of my own father. As far as he was concerned, every day without progress forward was a day walking backwards. Or that's what he liked to tell us.

"Well, Rachel, I stopped by at the beginning of the week and everything was working perfectly." As if to prove his point he walked to the front door and flipped the noisy light switch. With a click, the horrible, cheap-looking light flicked on the wall near the door. He flipped it a few times like a pushy kid, and I swore to myself that I would not tell him off.

"Well, I'm not sure why it wasn't working this morning. I haven't heard of any reports of outages or anything else.

But it's on now, and that's all that matters. Despite this minor setback, we did get the doors labeled, and I can go ahead and set up our computers. Did your wife receive the list of suggested paint colors for the four parlors?" I smiled as I sat behind the only table in the place. The computers were boxed beside it. This wasn't the room we'd planned on working in, but I could tell that I needed to look busy.

"So you say you've walked through the house already?"

"Yes, I have." I continued to smile like a demented clown. "We've also completed some video documentation already (*shoot, why did I mention that?*) and marked the doors with signs to direct the contractors. Enjoy these quiet moments now, sir, because this place is about to be rocking."

He peered at me and said, "Come with me. I want to show you something." My smile faded quickly. I didn't feel threatened or unsafe, but his voice had that familiar *you're in trouble, young lady* sound to it that I'd heard from my father. Fortunately for me, he was out of the picture now.

"Sure, let me grab a notebook."

"You won't need it," he called back to me. He was halfway up the stairs already. For a sixty-year-old, Desmond Taylor had ninja skills. He was slightly bowlegged, had a head full of salt-and-pepper hair and was probably fifty pounds heavier than he should have been. His wife was twenty years his junior, and I liked her. So far. Things could change at any moment, though. Especially if she insisted on choosing paint colors that weren't on the list I sent. People always showed their true colors during a renovation. I'd discovered that from experience, although working for Carrie Jo and Ashland was my dream job. I knew they were just regular folks, but time and time again they'd proved how big their hearts were.

"I walked around looking for you two earlier, and that's when I found this. Is this someone's idea of a joke?" He pointed to one of the taped signs. There was a small, bloody palm print on the bottom of it, right where you couldn't miss it. The red liquid had dripped down the dirty wooden door.

"What? How did that get there? I swear, Mr. Taylor, that wasn't here earlier. No way would I do something like that. Ever." I tugged at the tape and pulled the sign off the door, and then I smelled the handprint. It didn't smell like paint or anything else. What did blood smell like? "Are there more?" I didn't wait for an answer but walked up and down the hall. I found that there were no more. At least not on this floor.

"Then how did it get here? Was this part of your video marketing? Because if it is, you should stop. That is not the kind of image we are going for here at Idlewood."

"Oh, gosh no! We don't do stuff like that. We are historians, not paranormal investigators, Mr. Taylor."

"I don't like this, Rachel. There has been enough said about this house over the years. I won't tolerate séances, ghost tours or anything like that. I heard a rumor today that your boss's company was involved in some supernatural goings-on at Seven Sisters. I repeat, I don't want anything like that here at Idlewood." I didn't say anything, just held the gross sign while he lectured me. "I'm sorry to sound like a mean old fart, but that's how I want it. All right?"

"Right, well, that's what we plan to do, sir. This is all a big misunderstanding."

"I hope what you're telling me is the truth. If your boss was here, I'd be telling her all this. But since she isn't, you get to hear it. Not such a fun job now, is it?" He relaxed a little but eyeballed the sign like he didn't believe me.

"I'd like to throw this away before it drips everywhere. Unless there is something else you'd like to show me, sir?"

"No, that's it. I don't mean to come off like a beast, but I just want to be clear. How am I going to rent this place out if people are afraid to come here? I hope that makes sense."

"Yes, sir. It does." I smiled again, and we walked down the wide stairs together. "I'll get to the bottom of this. Someone's idea of a prank, I suppose." Speaking of pranks, now was as good a time as any to ask about our earlier visitor. "Which reminds me, did you hire an electrician named Angus?"

"My wife and your boss have taken care of all the hiring. There could have been an Angus in the bunch. Why?"

"Oh, just curious. Thanks for stopping by, Mr. Taylor. Is there anything else I can help you with?"

"Nope. I'll head out, since everything is working here. Too bad I didn't get to see Mrs. Stuart. Well, maybe tomorrow. I'll stop by then."

"She might be here, but I don't think I will. Tomorrow is Saturday."

"Oh yeah. Well, I'll see you ladies on Monday. If there's anything else you need, just let me know."

"Will do, sir." I smiled at him as he left out the front door. I breathed a sigh of relief. Nope. CJ didn't pay me enough to handle angry homeowners—and bloody handprints. I shoved the paper in a plastic bag. Gross. Who would do such a thing? Not me. Not CJ. Was there any possible way that Angus character could have done it? Who knew? I sure didn't.

I tore my eyes away from the plastic bag and tossed around some ideas. The thing to do now was take my mind off of it, but I'd have to stay a little while. I wouldn't put it past Desmond Taylor to come back for round two. I'd sure as heck be out of here before dark, though. I didn't care if the pope himself stopped by. I decided to set up the wireless router. Imagine having Internet run in a place like this.

Just to be sure, I went back to the light switch and flipped it a few times. Yep, now everything was golden. So weird that it wasn't working earlier. I looked along the baseboards of the front room to see if I could trace the DSL line. Not in here. That was good. We'd planned on working in one of the front parlors. I walked to the right and noticed a business card on the floor. I bent down to pick it up. Just a plain old business card with a name and phone number on it. No bloody fingerprints, thank God.

Angus McGarrity.

Well, how many Anguses could a girl meet in one day? I rubbed my finger over the name. So he wasn't a ghost. He was as real as I was. That was a relief, but I wondered why he disappeared earlier without so much as a "Goodbye, y'all." I shoved the card in my pocket and went back to work. What a day, and it wasn't even lunch yet! I got busy moving the table in here. I dragged the heavy thing, hating the noisy sound it made. The echoes were unbearable in here. I hated echoes now.

La-la-la... I hummed in my head. I wasn't going to think about that voice. Nobody was repeating my words because I refused to say anything. What did Mr. Taylor expect? That I would stay here all day by myself? Was he coming back by?

Oh my God! I was here by myself! *La-la-la...not going to think about it.*

Just then I heard the familiar child's voice. It came from above, no. It was behind me. No! All around me!

Rachel Kowalski...

"Who's there?" No response. The stillness was almost as bad as hearing my name on the lips of an invisible spirit. Oh my gosh! This thing knew who I was!

"Is this some sort of joke, Carrie Jo?" No way was it her, but I had to try and calm my mind. I dug in my pocket for my phone. Now who would I call? Carrie Jo was sleeping. The rest of the team wasn't scheduled to be here until next week. It was just me and the echo. I could call Chip and fake an IT question, but then he'd want to come over. I couldn't handle that. He would definitely assume that any contact from me was my way of asking him to come back. I'd rather let the ghost kid get me than do that. I liked Chip, but his mother? Not so much. The both of them together was just too much. I felt the card in my pocket. I read the phone number and called Angus McGarrity.

It was worth a shot. Anything was better than being at Idlewood alone.

"Hi? Angus? I don't know if you remember me, but I'm Rachel. We met earlier at Idlewood. Right...Katie Holmes..." *Hmm...minus ten points for the Katie Holmes reference.* "I was wondering if you wouldn't mind coming back out." Now what did I tell him? I couldn't just say, "I'm afraid of the echo."

Suddenly, as if it read my mind, the light switch began to pop off and on. The noisy clicking sound echoed through the bare foyer. "I've got an electrical short, I think..." I stared at the switch, watching it flip off and on. *How in the heck?* "Yes, now, please. It's kind of important. Okay, I'll see you soon." I hung up the phone, and the clicking stopped. I couldn't run out the front door, because that was where the switch was. Instead, I slowly made my way toward one of the French doors in the parlor behind me. At least that had been the plan.

Until the shadow swept by me, sending a chill over me. Then I ran to the front door with all my might.

Chapter Seven—Carrie Jo

"Where is she? Where is that homewrecker? I'm going to…"

"Whoa, CJ! She's gone, and she's not coming back. There is no home wrecked here. I'm sorry you had to see her act like that. I swear she's never done anything like that before."

"Sure," I said, rubbing the lump on my head.

"All I wanted to do was surprise you—not like that, of course."

I swung my feet over the side of the couch and caught the damp washcloth that fell off my head. It wouldn't do any good for a possible concussion, but that was Ashland's universal medicine: ice packs and damp cloths. "Surprise me by bringing another woman into my house?" I wasn't sure I was ready to let this go. It all seemed so strange. So surreal.

He said slowly, as if I had lost my senses, "She helped me bring in the stuff I picked up for my surprise dinner for you. I had some boxes, a few gifts I got you. I had no idea she was going to lay one on me."

I rolled my eyes at the idea of him giving me gifts. That seemed to be Ashland's go-to move when he knew I was ticked at him. Another trait I normally loved, but not so much today. "No idea, huh? And I'm the bad guy when I asked you earlier if you two discussed our marriage."

"And we never have. Sure, she's asked a few nosy questions, but I never gave her any information about us. I guess she assumed that because she and I had been spending so much time together, because I've been away from home so much recently, I wanted her. But I don't. I want you, Carrie Jo. I realize I'm not the guy I used to be—I mean, we've taken a beating financially—but it's going to get better, I promise."

I gave him a wimpy smile. Ashland sounded so vulnerable, so lost. It wasn't until that moment that I realized how much his identity had been tied up in his financial status. And his old name. He'd lost most of his money (or rather, given it away) recently, and his family name had surely been tarnished. But I didn't care about those things. Surely he knew that. "I love you, Ashland. You, not your name or your money."

"I know that," he said, but I could tell I struck a nerve. He reached for my hand and held it for a minute. "I had no idea I was married to such a thug," he added with a small smile.

"Ha! Not much of one. I'm the one that got knocked out."

Now it was his turn to laugh. "She's the one that ran out the door. I think she was worried about what you'd do when you woke up. But you do have a nasty lump, babe."

"Ugh, I can feel it. What is it about new house projects that makes me want to knock myself out. It's getting kind of old. Maybe I should become a Tupperware saleslady or something. Who knew historians led such dangerous lives?"

"Seriously, CJ. I need to take you to the hospital or at least to an urgent care. You might have a concussion. That was a nasty fall."

I liked how he put that. A fall. Not a punch in the face. "Oh, great. What does my face look like?" I went to the mirror in the entryway and examined myself. I didn't see much on my face, just a small bump on my forehead that I could easily hide with my bangs. And I had a few scratches on my arms. I couldn't believe for the first time in my life I was involved in a "catfight." Boy, Detra Ann was going to get a kick out of this.

"Her face was worse than yours. I can't believe all this happened. I'm really sorry, babe."

"Oh my God! The baby! What time is it?"

"I'll go get him. And then we'll go to the urgent care." He was out the door before I could argue with him. I barely had time to fill my ice pack when someone started banging on the front door. I wasn't expecting anyone.

"Ma'am. Please open the door. This is Officer Stone from the Mobile Police Department."

Pressing the bag to my forehead, I padded to the door and opened it, surprised to see two police cars in my narrow driveway. "May I help you?"

"Carrie Jo Stuart?"

"Yes?" I asked cautiously. I was getting a bad feeling about this.

"May we come in?"

"Um, sure."

The young officer stepped in, his silent partner behind him. "As I said, I am Officer Stone, and this is my partner, Officer Davies. We're here following up on a report we've received from a Miss Stevenson. Apparently you assaulted her earlier, and the victim is pressing charges against you. Would you mind coming with me?"

Was he kidding me? "Yes! I *would* mind coming with you! Look at my head. Did Miss Stevenson happen to tell you where this alleged assault took place? Here—in my house! I'm afraid Miss Stevenson isn't telling the whole truth, Officer."

"She says she came to the house at the request of your husband and together you two assaulted her. Miss Stevenson alleges that you punched her in the face when she refused your husband's advances. I'd like to talk to him too. Do you know where I can find him?"

"What?" I gasped. I could hardly believe what I was hearing. "That is disgusting! We aren't freaks! She attacked me!"

Up until that moment I half believed Officer Davies was on my side. She wasn't now, for sure. "Ma'am, husbands do a lot of things that wives don't know about. I'm sure your husband is no exception. Now if we could just take that short ride, I am sure we can get this all straightened out."

"You sure are sure about a lot, Officer. What you said might be true for a lot of husbands, but not mine. He's gone to pick up our son from day care. He'll be home in a few minutes. If you wouldn't mind waiting, I am certain we can clear this all up. This is unbelievable!"

"We'll wait, then. Do you need medical attention, Mrs. Stuart?"

I hadn't planned on going to urgent care or anywhere else, but now that Libby was making such ridiculous allegations, I might as well get it all on record. "Yes, in fact that was where we were going when Ashland got home. If you don't mind, I'd like to go change my clothes before we leave. Unless you think I'll crawl out an upstairs window." Officer Davies didn't appreciate my sarcastic tone. She pushed her hat up and stared at me sternly. She had narrow brown eyes and a bad haircut. Some things a hat just couldn't hide.

"Allegations of assault are no laughing matter, ma'am. We take these charges very seriously. I'll be happy to escort you upstairs so you can change."

I sat on my couch and pushed the ice pack to my head. "No thanks, I think I'll skip that, but I would like my cell phone and my purse. It's in the guest room. Just down the hall." *There you go, officer-lady. Fetch my stuff.* Officer Davies left with a sneer and came back in less than ten seconds like she was going to miss the part where they beat me with rubber hoses. I pretended I didn't notice that she'd rifled through my Michael Kors handbag. I picked up my cell phone and began tapping a message when she interrupted me.

"You make a habit of staying in your guest room, or do you hang out in there just on special occasions?" Her insinuation embarrassed her partner and me. Since it wasn't really a question, I didn't answer her. Officer Stone shuffled his feet and looked at the pictures of Ashland on the mantelpiece.

"Hey, I know him. That's Ashland! I thought I recognized the name, but you can't mistake his face, can you? I didn't know he got married. Congratulations, ma'am."

"Thanks," I said, wincing as I adjusted the ice pack. "Shoot!"

"We used to play head-to-head during football season. I played quarterback for UMS. I can't tell you how many times Stuart handed me my ass. I mean, roughed me up. Excuse me. Man, he was good. I wish I'd played half as well as he did. Everyone was sure he'd go to 'Bama or LSU."

I smiled suddenly. "Are you Tim Stone? The guy with a head like a rock? Ashland has mentioned you a time or two before."

Officer Stone stood proudly with his hands on his hips, rocking back and forth on his heels. He grinned even bigger, pointed at my head and said, "Yeah, no offense, but I've taken much bigger whacks to the head than that."

"No offense taken."

"Wow, it's going to be good to see him. I mean, well, it would be." Officer Davies gave him a warning look, but he ignored her. "If you don't mind, may I sit?" I nodded, and he made himself comfortable in the oversize occasional chair beside me. Flipping out his notebook he said, "Maybe we can clear this up without putting y'all through the ringer, unless she absolutely insists on pressing charges. Can you tell me your side of the story?"

"I'm going out to wait on the husband," Officer Davies said as she stomped out of the room.

"Fine. Now, Mrs. Stuart, tell me what happened. You came home and found them together?"

"No, I was already here. You see, Ashland and I are new parents, and I took baby AJ to day care."

He slapped his leg and said, "No way! He's a dad?"

"Pretty good one too. Anyway…" I told the officer the whole sordid story, and he scribbled down notes as I spoke.

"Stevenson…Stevenson…where do I know that name from?"

"Well, she's Jeremy Stevenson's sister, and Jeremy used to play ball with Ashland at Mercy. Maybe you know him from there?"

"Yeah, I remember that kid. He wasn't as good as Ashland, but he wasn't bad. Her I don't remember at all, but that's nothing surprising. I had a steady girl myself in school, so I wouldn't have been looking around. You know, until today I would never have taken Ash as that kind of guy either."

"He's not at all."

"Tim? What's going on, buddy?" Ashland finally arrived, immediately looking protective but unsure of the current situation. No doubt he'd met the charismatic Officer Davies already. Baby Ashland slept on his shoulder. My head hurt, but I couldn't resist holding baby AJ. It felt like I hadn't seen him in three days. I kissed his puffy pink cheek and held him close. He was what my old friend Bette would have called a "lump of love." I was so happy that he was sleeping through all this.

"Oh, nothing much. On the force now. Been with them for about three years. I see you've done pretty well. Gotten hitched, and you're a dad. What's this kiddo's name again? AJ? Future quarterback, huh?" He touched the baby's clenched fist and spoke softly to him. I could have liked this guy if he hadn't threatened to lock us up for trying to assault Libby.

"No offense, Stone, but we can catch up later. Why do I have police cars in my driveway?"

"A Miss Stevenson filed a complaint against the two of you. I'm here to investigate and determine whether or not we should arrest y'all for, well, assault, for one thing."

Ashland's face said it all. Officer Stone kept talking, nervously explaining the allegations. He ended with an apology. "You know I'm just doing my job. If I had known it was you to begin with, I wouldn't have been so hasty about stopping by, but there are a ton of Stuarts out this way. I'll tell my partner there's nothing to all this. I'm sure y'all can work it out without going to the courthouse."

To my surprise my husband shook his head emphatically. For the first time in a long time, he swore too. "Hell no! I want to file a complaint against *her*. She behaved inappropriately, my wife called her on it, and Libby attacked her. Plain and simple. Carrie Jo was just defending herself. Before I could stop her, she knocked my wife out and ran out the door. I don't have any idea how she got home or what she did after that. I had to pick up my son, and then I was going to take Carrie Jo to urgent care. Which I should do right now."

"Actually, we've got an ambulance en route now, at your wife's request." His radio squawked to life. "What's that?"

"Ambulance is here," Davies croaked over the scratchy speaker.

"All right, can you walk okay, Mrs. Stuart?"

"Yes, but please call me Carrie Jo."

"Okay, let's get you checked out, Carrie Jo. Then my partner and I will go pick up Miss Stevenson." To Ashland he whispered, "You know how these attorneys are. She's going to hit the roof when I arrest her. You sure you want to do that?"

"Yeah, I'm sure. I'm not afraid of her."

Officer Stone shook his head and walked me out to the ambulance. I handed baby AJ to my husband and let the paramedics poke on my head for a few minutes. Of course they wanted me to go to the hospital, and of course I refused.

"I'll be fine."

"Well, no sleeping for eight hours, but I'm pretty sure this little guy will make sure you stay awake." The EMT smiled at baby AJ, who was now waking up and seemed very interested in what she was doing. "And you watch her, sir. If she gets the slightest bit nauseated or dizzy, march her up to the hospital. No arguments. A concussion is nothing to play with."

The ambulance drove away, and we watched with relief as the police emptied out of our driveway. I wanted to wave at the neighbors who'd stepped outside to watch the hullabaloo, and I groaned as Astrid strutted our way. I heard Ashland sigh too.

Thank goodness Detra Ann and Henri drove up. Astrid turned awkwardly and went back to her house. For some reason she didn't care for our best friends too much. Someday I'd find out why.

Chapter Eight—Rachel

It was Saturday afternoon, and I'd been helping Gran tidy up the garage. Mom was working double shifts at the diner, and helping out was the least I could do. I mean, we did live with her. She was finally giving up her collection of vinyl records, and we were busy sweeping the big empty space one last time.

"Yep, this is going to be perfect," she said as she perused the near-empty garage.

I stashed the broom in the tiny broom closet and nosily flipped through the dusty records. Who the heck was Shaun Cassidy? Nope. Nope. Ooh…Sinatra. I might keep that one. "What's perfect, Gran?"

"Your new apartment."

"What?" I said with a laugh.

"This space is going to be yours. You're a grown woman, and you need privacy. And I need the room you're in. I've got plans."

I could hardly believe what I was hearing. She was ditching her vinyls and making plans, all in one day? This was unheard of. I had to get to the bottom of it. "Gran, I can't let you do that. And I'm perfectly happy with my room. If this is about me moving out…"

"I don't want you to move out. I like having my family around, but I'm kicking you out of that room for two reasons. First, because you snore like a freight train and the wall between us is paper thin and secondly, because you are a young lady now and you need your privacy. You should be able to have someone over without worrying about the noise you two might make."

"Gran! I would never."

"Oh, please. I'm your grandmother. You don't think I thought you and Big Ears were playing tiddlywinks in there, did you? Besides, how do you think you got here?"

"Yuck! Can we talk about something else?" She smiled wickedly and headed to the door that led into the house. "Renovating this room for me is too much. I can't let you do that. Not for me."

"Let me? I've got blue jeans older than you. I don't need your permission, Rachel. It's a done deal. The construction crew will be here Monday. They will have it all prettied up in a few days, and you'll be good to go. You can even pick out the paint color. But for goodness' sake, no purple. That color just irks me." I knew why. It irked me too.

"All right, Gran. If you're determined to do it."

"I am. Now come inside and get your shower. You stink, and it's almost time for your date."

I smiled at her generosity. Sometimes she could be a real crank pot, and other times she did something like this. I loved Gran's unpredictability. It drove my mother crazy, but I loved it. When I was a kid, I used to tell her, "I want to be you when I grow up." I watched her walk away and said, "Hey! You never told me what you're using the old room for."

"No, I didn't, did I?"

"Oh boy," I said as I put Frank Sinatra's record back in the bin and returned it to the pile. The Salvation Army truck would be here Monday to haul this stuff away. In a way, I was going to be a bit sad to see it all go, but when was I going to ride that bike again or play with that old doll-house?

Dollhouse. That reminded me of Idlewood. There was one in the attic space. I wish I'd taken a look at it before I ran out of there like a scaredy cat. Gran was wrong, my date was two hours away, but I showered, changed and sat in front of my computer to kill some time.

I remembered the search engine Henri told me about. A few mouse clicks later, there I was on Haunted Web, the place to go when you wanted to track down a spirit. Or at least the reports on one. Then I remembered the promised list, opened the email from Henri and began scanning through the hits. Most were incomplete and some were copies or partial copies of useless reports with sketchy details. But there were some interesting things about the old house and its most troubled and famous family, the Fergusons. The article that drew my attention was the one that Henri mentioned in his email.

Idlewood Plantation in Mobile, Alabama, has many secrets—including the location of two Ferguson children who disappeared on or around the property in the 1870s following the death of their oldest sister, fifteen-year-old Tallulah Ferguson. The house has been closed to the public for many years, but older reports suggest the spirits of the 'lost children' manifest as shadowy figures in certain parts of the house, and the sounds of children crying have been said to "freeze your blood," according to former employee Beatrice Overton.

I glanced at the publication date. Hmm...this was published in 2000. I wrote down the reporter's name and a few other notes from the article. I scrolled down past the historical stuff—I had a good grasp on that. Was I jumping the gun here? Could my desire to be treated like an equal at the office be driving me to hunt for ghosts where there weren't any? I frowned at the screen. The house might not even be haunted. Gran said that sometimes things followed you. Was it possible that "someone" from Seven Sisters followed us to Idlewood? I'd called Carrie Jo last night to tell about the power and give her an update on Mr. Taylor's general attitude. She wasn't too worried about it, and I decided to adopt her approach. And I decided not to tell her anything about the bloody handprint or anything else.

Here is the transcript from my interview with Beatrice Overton: "My employers, I don't think they would like me to mention their names, they were very strict about what rooms we used. They didn't like you to wander around too much because of all the work that needed to be done. In the beginning, we stayed only in the rooms at the front of the house, but they were young and quite handy with tools. Such a lovely couple. They had big plans and even got a grant from the city to restore Idlewood to her former glory. I really liked them. So thoughtful, and they didn't mind that I had a son of my own. I didn't do much at first except help the missus with her baby, bring them iced tea, prepare the meals, do some light gardening. That first year all was quiet, all was peaceful, but then they began work upstairs. Juliet—oh goodness. I wasn't supposed to tell you her name. But I expect you could find out if you really wanted to anyway. Well, Juliet began to have disturbing episodes where she would cry for a solid hour. I couldn't blame her. She was expecting their second child, but the pregnancy went wrong and she lost the baby. Yes, she cried so much then. And then the children would cry. It was like a blanket of gloom was tossed over the whole place.

"One afternoon, I heard her in her room. The second room on the left at the top of the stairs. Her husband, Mr. Gary, he had to go to Shreveport—I think he was glad to go because he couldn't put a foot right. His mother passed away, and he had to clear out her old place. Well, Juliet was crying again, just sobbing like her poor old heart was broken in pieces. The baby, a precious little gem he was, he was tired and ready to take his afternoon nap. I'd gotten his room nice and cool with the standing fan and laid him down to rest in his crib. I passed Juliet's room again and heard her pitiful voice, crying over that baby. I heard her whispering, mumbling, and the sound of it made the hair stand up on my arms. I felt terrible but didn't bother her. I had said all I could to cheer her. It was up to her now. I turned on the baby monitor, put it in my apron pocket and went about tidying the downstairs kitchen. About ten minutes later I heard a strange squeaking noise coming from the baby monitor, like someone was moving an old desk around. You know, one of those heavy ones that the schoolmarms used to sit behind. Maybe you don't know. Life is different back in England. Well, just then, guess who walked in through the back door? Juliet! She was carrying a big basket full of vegetables. She scared me nearly out of my skin! That was when we heard the most terrible sound coming from the baby monitor. It was as if someone had turned the volume all the way up. It squealed like an old radio on the wrong station. Then it said her name!

"She dropped the basket, and those vegetables rolled everywhere. I remember those turnips were so large. They clunked on the floor like baby doll heads." Ms. Overton shivered here.

"We ran up those stairs, taking them two by two, until we got to the boy's room. His name was Christopher. Such a delightful, happy baby he was. We couldn't get the door open at first, and Juliet and I screamed and banged on it. I don't know why; the child couldn't open it. But someone had to be in there! We could hear the furniture moving and heard this strange banging noise.

"*Whack, whack, whack!*

"*All I could think about was the poor baby. That poor baby and those turnips. I don't know why I thought about such a thing, but I did. Then the child began to cry for his mother, and the door opened. We fell into the room and saw the strangest thing. The crib had moved ten feet, and one side of the crib was up on the windowsill. Now let me tell you something: there is no way that baby could have done that. That sill was at least a foot off the floor. That baby, and he wasn't even two yet, there was no way he could have crawled out of the crib, lifted it up onto the sill and crawled back in it. Someone had been trying to push that baby's bed out the window! But there was no one else in that room. The glass was cracked, and the babe was inconsolable. So were we all! Juliet took that baby and left the house, and as far as I know she never came back. I stayed downstairs and only went back up when it came time to pack everything away. Now mind you, I didn't stay there at night. I had a friend on Hunter Avenue. My boy and I spent three months on her couch until I helped Mr. Gary close up the house and he helped me find new employment. Oh, but it was a terrible thing. I never wanted to work in a big house like that again.*"

A knock on the door of my room made me jump out of my chair.

"I think that young man is at the door, Rachel, and I doubt he's here for me."

"Okay, Gran! Thanks!" I glanced in the mirror and sighed. Where had the time gone? I looked messy, but I had my mother's nice eyes and Gran's sassy smile. That was all I needed.

I practically ran down the stairs to answer the door. What was I doing inviting a near stranger to my home? This was so unlike me, but there was something about Angus. Something hidden. Something interesting. Despite the fact that I now knew he was entirely real and not a ghost, I wanted Gran to "scan" him. I valued her opinion.

And that was when the trouble really began.

Chapter Nine—Carrie Jo

The phone rang a number of times, but we chose not to answer it. It would just be the neighbors wanting to make sure we were "all okay." Or more to the point, they wanted to know what was going on over here. That was the downside of living in this tightknit community—inquiring minds always wanted to know. The only time I did answer the phone was when my mother called. I had to give her the rundown, and she didn't seem surprised by any of it. I got the impression she wasn't that pleased with Ashland, but then again, she didn't trust men in general. She let me know that she'd be back in Mobile in a few days. She had her property squared away and was ready to make a new life with us. And, she informed me, there'd be no day care for AJ. She'd keep him for me. I felt my back bristle at that, but I kept my mouth shut. At least for now. I'd learned to pick my battles.

Despite her pushiness when it came to her grandson, I was glad she was coming back. It was nice to have my mother in my life, and baby AJ loved her. To avoid further interruption, I turned off the ringers on all the phones. Our best friends hung around for a few hours, and we made quick work of the spiral ham and tasty sides Doreen had left for us. Detra Ann and I tidied up the kitchen and she continued to pepper me with questions. I was ready to talk about something else but was too polite to say so.

We joined the guys in the living room, and I hunkered down on the comfy couch next to Ashland.

"Has she lost her mind? Why would she make a move like that right here in your house, CJ?"

"Isn't it obvious?" Henri piped up, sounding a little snappy. He'd been quiet up to now. I was beginning to wonder if we'd ticked him off somehow.

"It's not obvious to me. What are you thinking?" Ashland rubbed his stubble and passed the red ball back to the baby. AJ thought throwing it over the side of the playpen was a hoot. I'd gotten tired of retrieving it, but my husband didn't seem to mind at all. I'd give him about a dozen more catches. Like me, he looked tired. I hadn't given it much thought, but I guessed all the travel was catching up on him.

"She's after a payday. And since she couldn't seduce you to get what she wanted, she'll eventually accuse you of sexual harassment. She had two options. Blackmail or file a lawsuit. Since CJ busted her, I would say the latter now. And I'm no expert, but I'd say Libby Stevenson is definitely the lawsuit kind of gal, being a lawyer and all. I wouldn't be surprised if you got served in the very near future." Henri tossed back the remnants of his drink. He was drinking the hard stuff tonight, Kentucky bourbon. He crunched the ice in his teeth and stared at us. For an uncomfortable moment nobody said a word. When the silence got strained enough, I piped in. *That's me. The old icebreaker.*

"What's up, Henri? We're your friends. You can tell us what's going on," I said to him point-blank. My gut instinct told me something was majorly wrong.

"Nothing. I'm fine," he replied with an empty smile.

Detra Ann burst into the conversation, "You *are* lying! I *know* you are, so stop it. What's really going on?"

With his elbows on his knees and his fists together under his chin, he looked like a deer in the headlights of an oncoming semi. His warm brown eyes were expressive and sad. "I don't want to talk about this right now. We'll talk later."

"No way! I want to know now. If it's that bad, I want our friends around. What is it, Harry? You're scaring me."

He rubbed his hands together and clapped them. Now he looked as uncomfortable as a prostitute in church, as Bette would say.

"I don't think I can get married until I know what happened to Aleezabeth."

"What?" Detra Ann asked, blinking at him.

"I made a promise to Lenore, and I haven't lived up to it. Not at all. Lenore gave her life for us. The least we could do is find out what happened to Aleezabeth. I love you, Detra Ann. I would never have asked you to marry me if I didn't. I *want* to marry you, but if we married right now I'd be bringing half myself. I don't want that for us, and you don't deserve that."

"Are you serious? After everything we've been through?"

"Sugar, it's *because* of what we've been through that I can say this. I love you. Please help me find out what happened to Aleezabeth so I can move on with my life—hopefully, if you still love me, we'll take that step together."

"What if we can't find her? What then?"

He sighed sadly. "I guess we'll cross that bridge when we come to it."

"I can't believe I'm hearing this." She had the baby between her legs on the floor. She'd taken him out a few minutes ago so he could roll the ball to Ashland rather than throw it across the room. She'd helped him retrieve the ball one last time, and he excitedly rolled it back to his Daddy and clapped his hands, oblivious to the escalating tension.

I felt desperate to preserve our happy family, so again I spoke up. "Detra Ann, I think what he's saying is…"

Her blue eyes widened and she said, "Please tell me you are not taking his side, CJ."

I ignored Ashland's warning look. In for a penny, in for a pound. "There are no sides here, Detra Ann. I think what he's trying to say is he needs closure. And we…"

"I love you to pieces, but this has nothing to do with you." She handed the baby to Ashland and kissed the squirming child's head. She stood up calmly and straightened her clothes. She was leaving, and she was ticked at both Henri and me now.

"I told you I wanted to talk about this alone, not in public," he began. *You are totally screwing this up, Henri.* I tried to send him mental cues. Too bad we weren't telepaths.

"You know what. I just want to go home. Be by myself for a while." She raised her manicured hand politely to stop him. "I'll drive myself, if you don't mind."

"No, take your time. I'll call you later."

"Or not. I'm okay either way." She grabbed her cashmere cardigan and leather purse and walked out the front door. At least she didn't slam it.

What was happening? "Go after her, Henri. Tell her you're sorry."

Ashland stood now and brought the baby to me. I knew what he was doing. Trying to shut me up, his subtle way of reminding me once again that this had nothing to do with me. "Carrie Jo...I think AJ is hungry."

"Then feed him. His cereal is in his bag." I stared at the closed door and wondered if I should go after her myself. For some reason I felt panic rise up within me. As if I would never see her again. Or she'd tumble back inside a bottle and might not quit until she drank herself to death. When TD died, she drank for months. Henri and all of us had to band together to help pull her out of that dark, dangerous place.

"Please, babe."

After another moment of hesitation, I walked back in the living room with the baby. I showed him the cereal bowl in the diaper bag, and he bounced up and down with joy. Yep, he was my hungry boy! I put him on my hip—funny how that felt so natural, like he'd always been there—pulled the plastic lid back and gave him a few pieces of his favorite cereal treat. He chomped on them with his two white teeth and quickly wanted more. I had to pop them in fast or else he'd bite me in the process, which he thought was hysterical. Me? Not so much.

We sat on the couch together. I put AJ beside me and propped him up with pillows to keep him from tumbling off the sofa. My son had absolutely no fear of heights or falling or anything else except sleep. He smiled through his snack, showing teeth and bits of cereal. It was amazing how much I loved that sweet face. His dimples appeared, those Stuart dimples, and I smiled at him despite the drama that was playing out in my living room. "Good boy, AJ. Eat up." I touched his patch of blond hair that my mother liked to call duck fuzz and rubbed his perfectly round head. I felt so blessed to have such a lovely, happy baby.

I quietly listened as Ashland tried to encourage his friend—without my help. "Henri, I let you down. I should have told you what I've been seeing, but I've been so tied up in my own world I just lost track of the important things like my family and friends. You are like family to us. Please let us help you. I'll be happy to look, and Carrie Jo can dream. Do you have something that belonged to her? Something CJ can use to see her for dream catching?"

"I have a picture of her. Will that work?" Henri seemed overjoyed to hear that we wanted to help. Ash was right. We were lousy friends. Henri dug in his wallet and wiped at his eyes with the back of his hand. He was awash with emotions. I wanted to throw my arms around him and then kick him out the door after Detra Ann.

"It might. You never know. I'll give it a try tonight." I accepted the worn photo and studied the serene face that stared back at me. What could have happened to her? "If I see or hear anything useful, I will let you know. I swear."

Henri nodded and said, "I hope I didn't just lose the best thing that ever happened to me. I love Detra Ann."

"She'll understand," I said with false sincerity. I was glad Detra Ann wasn't here to witness my lie. I wasn't too good at it. I didn't know what would happen. Not now or anytime. All I could do was dream about the past—only once had I seen the future. AJ began to fuss and reach for the photo. I put a piece of cereal in his damp hand instead. I stared at the picture some more, and with ninja speed AJ snatched it from me.

"No, baby AJ! That's not yours." His bow lips curled up in a cry, and he reached for the picture again. I slid the photo in my back pants pocket and noticed a whiff of something putrid. "Excuse me, y'all. Baby bomb here." If Henri hadn't been here, I would have foisted the job on Ash, but it wasn't to be. I took the baby, a diaper and a pack of his wipes to the other side of the room behind the loveseat. I probably should have given them some privacy, but I was nosy like my neighbors. I had to know what was happening.

"I do see Aleezabeth, but she's with someone," Ashland said in a near whisper, as if he were seeing her right now. Maybe he was. "What's weird is I don't think he's a ghost. I mean, I don't know that she is either…I'm sorry I said that."

"No apologies needed. I've come to terms with the fact that she's dead, but I have to know what happened. She deserves to be vindicated if there is any wrongdoing involved."

"It's like he's not all visible, so I can't really see his face clearly. That might mean that he's still alive and not yet a spirit or that he's at rest. I'm not really sure," he confessed. I listened to it all, the hair on my arms creeping up as I endured AJ's unpleasant gift. Thankfully the baby didn't wrestle with me. It was like he was listening too. "Yes, she's close to you, like she knows you want to find her. She's showing me him again. Hmm…that's interesting. He's about your height, but I can't see any of his features. She's doing this now." Ashland made a motion across his upper lip. "Gosh, I wish I could hear her, but I can't. I think she's trying to say he has or had a mustache. Wait. Something about music. What is that? I think it's a saxophone. Yes, she's with a man who plays the saxophone. Or she was. Does that mean anything to you?"

Henri gasped and said, "Yes, I think so. She's talking about my father, her uncle. He must know something about what happened. He disappeared not long after she did, but I just assumed he ran out on us. Trevor, my father, he had a knack for leaving when times got tough. I never put the two together. Oh God! I hope this doesn't mean he was involved. I don't even know if he's still alive. I haven't seen him in over twenty years." He was crying now. Ashland sat beside him, saying nothing, just resting his hand on Henri's shoulder. Darn! Why had Detra Ann cut out of here so early? She would have learned so much. I was disappointed in her, but I would never tell her that. Unless she asked me. Then I wouldn't be able to lie about it because she'd know.

Well, we had a clue at least. A place to start, and we were one step closer to getting them in front of that altar. I wish he'd just have told us how he felt instead of telling her that he was having second thoughts. Or whatever you called it. I wrapped up AJ's stink bomb, put him in the playpen and dropped the diaper in the kitchen garbage can.

I closed the garbage can and grabbed the can of deodorizer. I sprayed the kitchen with the vanilla scent, hoping it would mask the smell of my foul baby.

Only the scent that came out wasn't vanilla. It smelled like an old perfume, Vanderbilt. Oh my gosh! It smelled like Lenore. Exactly like her. I stared at the label. It plainly said vanilla, and I'd used it many times before. No, this wasn't a mistake.

Lenore was making her presence known, but in a sweet, comfortable way.

She loved Henri, but she was holding her cousin to his promise. He wasn't lying. He had to find Aleezabeth now. The spirits were tired of waiting. They wanted to rest now.

Time to put Aleezabeth and Lenore to rest.

Not just for the dead but for the living too.

Chapter Ten—Rachel

How quickly the weekend flew by! Just like Gran promised, the construction crew was pulling in the driveway as I left for work Monday morning. All I could do was shake my head at the idea of such a project. Gran's generosity was humbling.

When I graduated from college I'd toyed with the idea of moving out into my own place; the Stuarts paid me well, despite their current situation. But Gran wouldn't hear of it. She liked having us around, and she wasn't the kind of woman who liked to control you. I had friends in and out of her house all the time growing up. That hadn't changed, but there weren't as many friends hanging out around the neighborhood anymore. Most of the young women my age were getting married, having babies and settling down into family lives of some sort or another. I wasn't in a hurry. And I'd never been in love.

But then I met Angus. He intrigued me, and I knew right from the get-go that Gran wasn't crazy about him. Which was also crazy, since she never disliked anyone. I guess that was the word for it. She wouldn't talk about it; in fact, when she finally came downstairs to meet him, she barely spoke. Yeah, it was weird. I apologized to Angus, but he didn't seem to notice that Gran was behaving strangely. Then again, how could he have known how she usually behaved? He was polite and friendly, and I liked him. Probably too much, too soon.

That first night we went for a walk around my neighborhood. Besides plenty of shade trees, there was a small park in the center of it that I loved to haunt when I could. I spent many a happy day hanging out with Julie and Karla on the swings. We called ourselves the "Swing Queens." We'd challenge each other to see who could swing the highest, and it was amazing fun until Julie's mother brought the hammer down on us. Of course that was after her daughter broke her arm falling from a ridiculous height. And it kind of freaked me out to see it. I never went that high on a swing again.

It was a warm evening, warmer than any we'd had so far this year, but some tidy homeowner was burning leaves somewhere so the air smelled like fall even though it was February. I adored the smell of burning leaves. We didn't hold hands or anything romantic, but it was exciting. We talked about how he spent his early childhood in the U.K., sometimes in Scotland, sometimes in London with his grandparents. He'd moved to the U.S. about four years ago, but he said Alabama felt like home.

"Really? How is that? It's got to be so different."

"When I was a child, I lived in Mobile for about two years. Short stay, but I went to Morningside Elementary, and I hated leaving those friends behind when it was time to go. I spent the rest of my life getting back."

"Were you able to reconnect with those old friends?"

"Not really. I was too young to remember a lot of their addresses or even their last names, but I'm glad to be here." We walked over to the swings. The poor old park was in such disrepair. It needed some attention for sure. Some of the swings were broken, and all of them were a bit rusty. We found two together and sat in them. "What about you? What's your story, Rachel? Where have you traveled?"

"I took a senior trip to Jamaica, and I've been to Natchez, Mississippi, about a half dozen times. My Gran loves going on those hokey plantation tours. I guess that's where I get my love for old places. And I've been to Pensacola, Destin and Gulf Shores for the beaches."

"You like the beach?" He smiled. "I can see that you do. Nice freckle patch across your nose."

"Hey—I like my freckles," I said lightly. "And yes, I love the beach. Don't you?"

"Red hair. Pale skin. The beach is not my friend."

I laughed at that. He would fry like a crackling if he spent any time on our local beaches. "I guess you'll have to restrict your visits to after the sun goes down. Kind of like a vampire."

He froze, his vivid blue eyes staring at me intently as he frowned. "I've been hearing jokes like that all my life. I don't find them funny." I stopped swinging and stared back. I was torn between apologizing and just leaving. Then he laughed. It was a head-thrown-back, full, throaty laugh. "I'm just kidding. You'll have to ignore my dark Scottish humor. I didn't offend you, did I?"

"No, I was worried that you had absolutely no sense of humor. That would definitely be a problem. I can't imagine dating—I mean being with—I mean being friends with someone who couldn't take a joke." Now that I had thoroughly embarrassed myself, I hid my face in my hands.

He touched my wrist. "Hey, I've got a sense of humor. In fact, I'm known far and wide for my pranks. Just wait until

April Fools' Day. As my friend, you'll get to experience my humor in creative ways."

"Oh Lord, that doesn't sound good."

After that, the "date" was very comfortable, and it was as if we'd known one another for years, not a few days. We both liked hard rock and had a mutual love for Celtic music. He was only twenty-five, but Angus was a certified electrician, a skill that developed from his love for puzzles. He enjoyed tracking lines and creating brand new electrical systems. We ended up grabbing some dinner at Hungry Howie's. We ended the night early, for a date, but I invited him to breakfast at my house.

Funny to think that after spending most of the weekend with him, I hadn't asked him why he'd left Idlewood so abruptly. I had to make a mental note to do so later. We had no plans to meet tonight. He said he was swamped with work, and so was I. Mr. Taylor was going to be a demanding client, but Carrie Jo handled him with her usual charm.

Mrs. Taylor—Cindy, as she insisted we call her—took a liking to me, apparently. She followed me around all morning, talking about the house and asking questions. She handed me back the paint color form, loaded with question marks and filled with notes. I tried to answer each question but in the end steered her away from hunter green and banana yellow for the parlors. I hoped this interaction wasn't a sign of things to come. This renovation would prove a nightmare if we had to stop every ten minutes to explain how and why we were going to do something.

When we had the opportunity, CJ and I exchanged "help me" glances. But the Taylors didn't stay long. Cindy let us know she'd be back at the end of the week to see how things were progressing. Better her than her perpetually ill-tempered husband. If she stuck to her word and came just on Fridays, I could live with that. Otherwise our carefully laid plans would be for naught. And that meant we'd be working weekends to catch up on our timeline.

I hadn't given much thought to the weird experience I'd had Friday, but now it looked like there was no avoiding going to the upper floors. The thing was to not go alone, I reminded myself.

Carrie Jo was on the phone with the mold guy, who apparently missed a few spots on the western side of the house. That was bad news for sure. That meant the plasterers and painters would have to wait. The painter assured her there was plenty of prep work to do and he could always take his crew outdoors until they got it straightened out. As she dialed another number, she mentioned Terrence Dale. We never had these problems at Seven Sisters. He'd taken care of everything, from finding good help to managing the timelines. I'd had a secret crush on the guy at the time, but he'd never shown me a bit of attention beyond his friendly, professional greetings. I'd cried for days before and after his memorial service.

"Hey, Rachel, could you show Darius the second-floor study where we want to put those bookcases? For some reason, my phone doesn't want to get a signal up there."

"Probably the range. Sure, I'll show him. Follow me." Darius didn't speak, and I could tell he didn't like being there. As we walked up the wide staircase together I said, "So, Darius, is your mother a big fan of biblical history?"

"What?" he asked, looking around him nervously.

"Biblical history. You know, Darius the Mede."

"No, I don't know much about the Bible, and I'm pretty sure she didn't either."

Okay, then. Note to self: Don't make small talk with Darius.

We took a left at the top of the stairs, I opened the first door we came to, and he followed me inside. It was cool up here. This room was completely bare; the walls had recently been plastered and skimmed, and the floors were stripped down, just waiting to be refinished. It felt like being inside a tomb. *That's a morbid thought, Rachel.* The fireplace was in the center of the far wall. The bookshelves were to go on either side of it, from floor to ceiling. Darius was supposedly a master carpenter and had come highly recommended by someone Ashland knew. I smiled pleasantly and waved my hands like I was some kind of game show hostess. "Carrie Jo wants the bookcases on either side of the fireplace. I think you got the mockups, right?"

"I drew them," he quipped. "Yes, I have the originals here." He tapped his leather portfolio. "I'd like to take measurements to make sure I have the numbers right before I start cutting. That's just how I do things." He glanced around. "I guess I'll have to go down for my ladder. Thought there might be one up here. Would you mind helping me? My helper is running late, and I need someone to hold the tape for me."

"Um, sure."

He laid his portfolio on the dusty mantelpiece and disappeared from the room quickly. Darius was all business, so I knew he wouldn't dawdle. I sure didn't have time for that today. I walked to the window. They were the tall kind with a high ledge, the kind the housekeeper had described in her account of the Idlewood ghost. I wondered if this was the very room where it all happened…

Mr. Taylor wasn't replacing these windows, since they'd been replaced after Hurricane Katrina. Thankfully they were exact replicas of the original windows, minus some warped glass and rotting wood. I glanced at my watch and leaned against the frame. The place was crawling with people, and trucks were everywhere. From here I could also see busy north Carlen street. Traffic moved smoothly for once, not bottlenecking like it could between traffic lights. I saw the bald-headed Darius open the tailgate of his truck and retrieve a green ladder and a tool bag. I glanced at my watch again. Darn, time was getting away from me. It was nearly noon.

I turned to walk away when I saw Angus on the property. I tapped the window like a goof. No way was he going to hear me from up here, and he probably wouldn't notice me in all the activity. I watched him weave through the overgrown hedges. Obviously he was coming to see me. Or coming to finish whatever he didn't finish the other day. A strange sense of worry crawled over me.

I couldn't run down the stairs and greet him. I needed to play it cool. I shoved my phone in my pocket and leaned my back against the wall with my arms crossed, totally forgetting about the Sheetrock and plaster dust. I heard footsteps approaching the room—these floors, although declared sturdy by our floor guy, had some give to them and liked to squeak in certain places. I wasn't too familiar with the various squeaky spots, but I heard Darius' work boots clearly. I never saw him walk past the door, but I heard the footfalls. Was it possible he forgot which room I was in?

"Hey, Darius! I'm in here!" I called out to him. The footsteps stopped, but I heard nothing else. "Darius!" I felt more flabbergasted by the second. He didn't answer me, and then the footsteps turned back as if he'd realized his mistake. But I hadn't seen him pass the door! It had to be someone else. Maybe Angus or one of a dozen others on the property today?

A sensible person would walk to the door and see who lingered in the hallway. A sensible person wouldn't hide in an empty room. There was nowhere to hide, anyway. The closet had no door and there were no curtains. Why did I feel like a child compelled to flee from an unknown monster?

"Who's there?" I had just enough courage to ask. The footsteps paused at the door, but nobody appeared. I stared, waiting for Darius to walk into the room. How long could it possibly take to come back with the ladder? I blinked at the emptiness and suddenly saw a figure. Or rather, the outline of a figure formed. A tall man, or something.

Whoever or whatever this was wanted me to see him. I knew that like I knew my own name. I held my breath in terror and watched the figure begin to fill in—the outline's edges were black, almost like someone had taken an eraser to an old photo. In a flash I saw the whole thing: a man wearing a vest, shirt and pants. His face was the picture of complete and utter hatred.

Don't belong! Leave, now!

Before I could call out or scream or do anything, Darius came whistling into the room, stepping right through the figure, and the shadow man disappeared. The carpenter set up his ladder in the corner and ignored my stupefied expression.

"You going to help me or what?"

"I'm sorry. I just remembered something. I'll send someone up. Sorry!"

I ran down the hall as fast as my ballet flats would carry me.

Chapter Eleven—Carrie Jo

Today had been one of those days that scurried past you and left you running after it. I'd spent a lot of time worrying about Detra Ann, but if she wouldn't talk to me, what could I do? She wasn't answering my phone calls, and I had the sneaking suspicion that my big mouth might have cost me our hard-fought friendship.

Henri kept the shop running, half expecting her to pop in the store any day. He'd made a number of calls to her mother, and she assured him that Detra Ann was fine and would be home soon. All he could do was wait for her. In the meantime, he'd put in some calls to relatives asking them about his father. Ashland and I stopped by the store last night, but Henri hadn't been in the socializing mood. I felt terrible that I'd not had any dreams about Aleezabeth. I vowed to try again tonight. I still had her picture in my purse, and I'd tried all weekend to summon up a dream about her.

My mother returned to Mobile and naturally wanted to watch baby AJ during the day. Ashland and I talked it over and opted to keep our spot at Small Steps but explained to the director that my mother wanted a little time with our son. We'd pay for his spot and wait for her to find a job, which she was always talking about doing. I cautiously allowed her back into my life and had to admit that my son loved her immensely and she him. At some point we'd have to do some heavy lifting in our relationship and tackle some tough subjects, but for now I enjoyed the maternal bliss.

When I got home Doreen had supper handled, the house had never been tidier and my son played happily in his bouncy swing. I tried to sneak in quietly, but as soon as I walked in he heard me and immediately began to cry. Yes, I had that effect on him.

"I'm coming, baby boy." I tossed everything on the table and waved at my mom as she came down the hallway with a dust mop. "Oh hi, Momma. He's better than a burglar alarm, isn't he?"

She laughed. "Only if you are the burglar. How was your day at the big house?"

"Great. We got so much done. Not." I smiled as I tried to pull my son out of the swing. "Wow, son. You must have gained ten pounds."

"He's a good ol' bag of rocks. Since you're home now, I'm going to take off. I've got plans this evening, and I need to clean up."

"Plans?" I smooched all over baby AJ.

"Yes, I'm going to the church at the corner. It's Monday Bingo!"

"Momma! How shocking! You playing bingo?" I half-joked with her. The mother I knew would never do something so "sinful." But she didn't think my comment was amusing at all. Her face crumpled, and she walked into the kitchen to put the broom away. I heard her and Doreen talking pleasantly, and I followed after her. "Momma, I'm sorry. I didn't mean to hurt your feelings."

"It's okay. I'll see you later. I have my key, and I won't be out too late." And she was gone. Doreen stared at me with wide eyes. She had no idea what was going on but was intuitive enough to know all wasn't right.

"I'm leaving too, Mrs. Stuart. I have tickets for the Saenger tonight, and I have an extra one. Have you seen 'Hello, Dolly!'? Would you like to go? It's playing all week. My daughter is in it!"

"No, I haven't, but I'd better hang out here. Monday kicked my tail, and I've got some things to do for work. Thanks for the invitation, though. And dinner smells wonderful."

"I made your favorite."

I kissed Ashland James on the top of his head again and chuckled. "You always say that, even if it's tuna fish. You know how much I *love* that."

The side door swung open, and my mom was standing there, her eyes wide, blood pouring down the side of her face.

"Oh my God! Momma! Doreen, take the baby! Go get Ashland!" My mother was wobbling—she was about to fall down the stairs. I grabbed her hand and threw her arm around my shoulder. I couldn't carry her to the dining room chair, so I helped her slide down to the floor. She was still conscious, but her eyes fluttered and the blood flowed. I grabbed a kitchen cloth and pressed it to her head. "Momma! Momma! What happened?"

"The man. I didn't see him until he hit me."

"Who hit you? Momma?" I watched in horror as my mother slumped over and her eyes closed. "Ashland!" I screamed as I scrambled to the wall and grabbed the house phone. I dialed 911 and immediately began giving the dispatcher the information she needed. The baby cried at the sight of his grandmother on the floor in a bloody heap, and

Ashland ran for fresh towels. "Doreen, please take AJ out of here. Can you two wait for the ambulance?"

"Okay," she said as she and AJ left us to tend to Momma. I laid my head on her chest and listened to her heart. I was no medical expert, but it didn't sound steady at all. "Ashland," I said, ready to cry.

"They're on the way. Here, let's use a fresh towel." As quick as he could, he swapped out the towels. I caught a glimpse of the wound now. It was at her left temple, in her hair. It looked like she'd been hit with something small, but the wound was deep. I had no idea what I was looking at.

"She said a man did it. I didn't see anyone when she came in. Do you think someone attacked her?"

"I don't know, babe. Hold the towel. I hear sirens."

Five minutes later, the EMTs were wheeling her out of our home and rushing her to nearby Springhill Memorial Hospital.

"Go with her. I'll follow in the car."

"Okay," I said as I scrambled into the ambulance after my mother's gurney. It seemed like the longest ambulance ride ever, but we finally made it to the hospital and then she was gone. I was forced to linger in the hallway with my bloody shirt and wait for someone to come see me. Nobody ever came, although a small army of medical folks constantly streamed by me. I finally sat on the floor and refused to go to the waiting room even though it was suggested to me a few times. I didn't cry, talk or bother anyone. I simply waited.

Ashland came in through the ambulance doors, bypassing the waiting room. He knew me. I wasn't one to wait when someone I loved was back here. I'd been here too much since I moved to Mobile. Far too much. "The baby?" I asked him.

"With Doreen. Listen to me, babe. I know you want to stay here so you can know what's happening, but you can't sit on the floor. Let's go to the restroom and clean you up. I've got you a fresh shirt to put on, and then I'll find out what's happening. I'll come to the waiting room, I promise." The Stuart name carried some weight in this hospital. His mother had given enough money to warrant a wing named after her. I did as he asked since I wasn't able to feel or think or anything else at the moment.

Momma's words played over and over in my mind. She said, "The man," not "a man." That was weird. I changed my shirt, tossed the old one in the garbage and cleaned the blood from my hands. My mother's blood. I stared at it as it washed down the drain. She'd left her home to be near me and baby AJ, and how did I thank her? By being a smartass, reminding her of her past. After I finished tidying up, I walked back to the waiting room and settled into a chair near a window. I stared out into the busy parking lot and waited for my husband to return.

"The family of Deidre Jardine?"

"That's me!" I said, jumping up. I was surprised to hear them call so quickly. But all they wanted was my mother's insurance information, which I didn't have. I did sign a form making myself responsible for her bills and impatiently plied the woman with questions, none of which she had answers for. She wasn't friendly, but I wasn't in the mood to care too much.

"Babe, come with me," Ashland called from the narrow hallway.

"We're not through yet," the hefty woman behind the counter said to me.

"I'll be back." I didn't wait for Miss Helpful's permission. I scurried out after Ashland. "What are they saying? What happened?"

"It looks like she was hit with some kind of projectile, like a rock. Sometimes gravel rocks from the driveways get in the road. Big trucks go by, hit the rocks just right and send them flying. Now if that is what happened, it would be an amazing freak accident, but it is not unheard of."

"Yes, but she said the man did it. She said nothing about a random rock."

"You and I both know how disorienting a head injury can be. She was probably talking out of her head and she never saw it coming. All we can do right now is speculate. They cleaned the wound and stitched her up. She's hurting, so they gave her some pain meds. I think they plan on keeping her overnight for observation. Standard procedure for a head injury."

"And she was awake? Why didn't you come get me?"

"I did. I'm here now."

I made an exasperated sound and pushed through the door into the room. "Momma?"

"She's resting right now. They'll be moving her up to the third floor when her room is ready. Are you her daughter?" Finally, a friendly face.

"Yes, ma'am, I am."

"Good, she was asking for you and your brother. I'm glad one of you made it so quickly." With a polite smile she grabbed her clipboard and walked toward the open door.

"Wait. I don't have a brother."

Her smile vanished, and she looked from me to Ashland as if this were some kind of joke. Consulting her clipboard, she read a note. "I wrote the names down. Umm...Carrie Jo and Chance Jardine."

"I'm Carrie Jo, but as far as I know there is no Chance Jardine."

She shrugged it off. "That's odd. I'll let the doctor know about this. I'll come back soon to help move her up to third."

Before I could question her further, she was gone and Ashland and I were left alone. I walked to my mother's bedside and watched her sleep. "Momma? I'm here. Can you hear me?" She didn't move a muscle, and I gazed down at her face as if I'd find the answer I wanted written in the tiny lines around her eyes. There were no answers there.

She was the picture of peace, except for the bandaged wound on the left side of her head. Her dark brown curls were shiny except for where the blood had dried and crusted. For the first time I could remember, she appeared frail and vulnerable. I wondered what she was dreaming about right now, if she dreamed at all.

And who in the world was Chance Jardine?

Chapter Twelve—Carrie Jo

"I spent my whole life trying to prevent this dream walking, to prevent it from developing in you, but I failed—and I caused you great pain in the process," my mother said earnestly. "Please believe me when I tell you that I begged God a hundred times to take it from us. To take it from you. If you had seen the things my mother went through...she got so obsessed. All she wanted to do was sleep, and then one day she didn't wake up. I think the dreaming killed her, and I didn't want that for you. I thought if I followed the rules, you know, went to church, lived a holy life, if I became pure in the eyes of God, I could save you. I can't explain my reasoning. It all seems so crazy now."

"I can't believe this." The pain in my back worsened, but I didn't move. I stared at her. "You mean you knew what was happening to me and you didn't tell me? You knew all this time? I thought I was crazy. I thought you hated me!"

"I'm sorry, Carrie Jo. I am very sorry that I let you grow up not knowing what I knew, even if that wasn't very much."

A blast of wind moaned around the eave of the house. I heard the television bleeping a weather alert in the other room, but I was frozen to the spot. Rachel and Detra Ann were upstairs, laughing about something. The surreal moment lingered and I said, "How could you do that?"

She wrung her hands and covered her mouth. Finally she said, "All I can say is I am sorry."

"And I'm supposed to do what now?" I stood up. "Act like a 'sorry' makes it all better. That it erases it all? You're wrong, Momma. I'm not going to forget and..." I felt the need to get away, but I wasn't done giving her a piece of my mind. Kind Carrie Jo warned me to watch my mouth—that I would regret it if I said something stupid—but as sure as I was pregnant, I didn't listen to the voice of reason.

"I'm not asking you to do anything, Carrie Jo. Nothing at all. It's up to you if you want to accept my apology or not."

My hands were clenched into fists. My ponytail felt limp and my back pain kicked into high gear, but the tears were coming. There would be no stopping them now. "With Ginny, you knew I wasn't crazy? And that time when I kept seeing that old man in my dreams—the one who hurt himself? You knew those dreams were real and you let me sleep in that house anyway?"

"We had nowhere else to go! It was that or the street. Your dad left us high and dry. I had to take whatever we could get." Her eyes narrowed in frustration. "I'm not proud of what I did, the decisions I made. Not proud at all. I know it's too late to ask you to trust me now, but I could not let one more day go by without telling you that I am sorry. I am sorry about it all."

"What about my father? How come you never wanted to tell me about him? You know what that's like when you're a kid? What it's like now? He hates me, doesn't he?" The pain in my back grew more intense, and I could see flashes of light around the corners of my eyes. I put my hand on the table to steady myself.

"No! No, Carrie Jo. He doesn't hate you. He was afraid of us. Afraid of me. He's not a bad man, just a fearful one."

Angry words were poised at the tip of my tongue, but they didn't spring forth like I wanted them to. To my surprise, a splash of water landed on the floor between my legs. It felt warm and sticky. It didn't stop. My sandaled feet were all wet now. All I could think to say was, "Momma?"

She jumped out of the chair. "It's okay, Carrie Jo. This is normal. Your water broke. The baby is coming soon. We've got to get you back to the hospital." She put her arm around me and led me to the side door. "Oh, shoot! My car isn't here. Detra Ann? Rachel?" The girls bounded down the stairs, still smiling until they saw me.

"Does this mean what I think it means?" Detra Ann asked.

"Yes, her water broke. We've got to get her back to the hospital right now."

"Why did they send her home? I knew that was a mistake. Let's take my car." She ran to the living room, grabbed her purse and came back. "Let's do this, CJ. You've got this! Rachel? Would you mind cleaning this up?"

"Sure, I'll clean up and turn everything off. I'll meet y'all up there. Should I call Ashland and Henri?"

"Yep, that would be great." I hated the way everyone was talking so calmly. Like one of us had a baby every day. "See you there. Oh, and grab her suitcase by the front door!" Detra Ann said as she hurried me down the steps.

"Can't I change my clothes first? I look like I peed on myself."

"Um, no, girl. You don't have time for that. Once your water breaks, labor could start any—"

Just then I screamed. If I thought yesterday's contractions were anything to brag about, I was sorely mistaken. "Shoot!

Shoot!" I said as I tried to remember how to breathe. I kicked myself again for not taking those Lamaze classes. "What do I do? What do I do, Momma?"

"Take slow, deep breaths when you can. I ain't gonna lie. It's gonna hurt like hell, but you'll survive."

"That's one hell of a pep talk, Deidre," Detra Ann scolded her.

"Well…. Oh, and don't push yet. For the love of God. It's not time to push. Let's get to the hospital first. We'll start timing the next one."

"Okay, okay," I said, breathing as slowly as I could. It was hard as heck to do with my heart pounding and my pulse racing. Detra Ann practically shoved me in the backseat and began backing the car down the driveway like a wild woman. *Should I tell her my purse is hanging out the door? Breathe, breathe, breathe!*

"Too bad it's not a girl. We could call her Jasmine, in honor of the storm," Detra Ann said, smiling at me in the rear-view mirror.

"Never," I promised her. "But Ashland would love that. I hope Rachel got a hold of him."

"Don't you worry about it, CJ. He'll be there." Detra Ann shouted at me as she ran a red light.

Deidre gasped and grabbed my hand. "Sweet Lord!"

"Get your watch ready. I feel another one coming. I'm sorry about your backseat, Detra Ann."

"Son of a b! Did you see that guy? I don't care about the backseat, but don't have the baby in my car! Jasmine deserves better."

Between pants and twists of pain I panted, "I'm—not-calling-her—Jasmine. Oh God, oh God!"

Detra Ann hit a curb trying to avoid a car. It was like being on a painful bumper car ride. My mother prayed beside me the whole time. Detra Ann grinned like a maniac when she wasn't honking at someone or threatening to cut their body parts off.

"Here we are! Pulling in the driveway now!" she yelled, forgetting once again that I was pregnant and not hard of hearing.

"Great! Perfect timing! Here comes another one!"

"Three minutes apart! That baby will be here soon!" My mother opened her door, rescued my purse and practically dragged me out of the backseat. "Hey! My daughter is having a baby! Like right now!"

"Momma! That's an ambulance guy. Not a nurse!"

It didn't matter. She was going to make sure someone helped me, and all I could do was hold my breath and hope the pain quit. A dark-haired young man squatted down in front of me. "What's your name?"

"Carrie Jo. It's Carrie Jo."

"Okay, Carrie Jo. I've got a chair here. Think you can stand so we can get you in it?"

"In just a second." I held my breath and waited for the contraction to let up.

"Don't hold your breath. Try to breathe through them. It will help with the pain. That's better. Take your time. I'll wait." Over his shoulder he told the approaching nurse what was happening.

"I think I can stand up now."

"They are three minutes apart," Deidre told the nurse as she pushed me through the hospital doors. "And her water broke."

"Sounds like we have a baby on the way. If it's a girl you could name her Jasmine."

I rolled my eyes at Detra Ann, who ran along beside me. "Never," I mouthed to her.

My clothes were drenched, my forehead was covered in sweat, and I was exhausted already. "Detra Ann, call Ashland, please. I need him here."

"I will. Deidre you stay with her while I find out what's going on."

Before I knew it, the nurse had me in the elevator and we were headed to the fifth floor. No long registration process for me. "Got no time to waste. The doctor says to bring you up now. Baby's coming! It's going to be okay. We're going to get you an IV started, he'll check to see how far you've dilated and then we'll go from there. How does that sound?"

"Like a dream. I'd like to wait for my husband."

The nurse, a young woman with pretty, soft-looking brown hair, smiled sympathetically. "Hopefully he will make it in time. But either way, I think you will meet your baby soon." Sure enough, another nurse came in quickly and had me rigged up to the IV in no time.

Dr. Gary arrived, apologizing that he had sent me home. A quick examination confirmed it. "Eight centimeters dilated. It's almost time."

"I know!" I practically screamed at him as another contraction, the strongest so far, took my breath away.

"How about an epidural to help with the pain?"

"Please? I would love one." All my pledges to "go natural" went out the window. I wondered if breast-feeding would hit the chopping block too.

"Be right back," Dr. Gary said as he pulled the blanket back down.

"Momma, please find out where Ashland is—he needs to get here."

Detra Ann walked back in, her phone in her hand. I could tell by the look on her face that something was wrong.

Something was dead wrong.

"Ashland is missing. Henri saw him fall in the water. He's with the authorities. They are looking for him now." She flew to my side and rubbed my hand. "You listen to me, Carrie Jo Stuart. We are not going to entertain anything negative about Ashland, you hear me? He is going to be fine. Right now, you have his baby to think about! I know you want to cry and fall apart, but you can't! You don't have that luxury! Let's have this baby so we can find out what's happening."

"Detra Ann, no! I can't—you have to go be with Henri! Help him find Ash! Please!"

Dr. Gary heard the shouting and came in; a nurse was tying on his face mask. "What is this? What's going on in here? Trying to have a baby, people."

"You don't understand, Dr. Gary. Carrie Jo's husband, Ashland, has disappeared off his boat. He's in the water and they haven't found him. But they will!"

"You had to tell her that now?" He sat on the rolling chair and rolled to my side. "I know you wish you could be doing something else right now, but this child needs you. Your son needs you. Let's welcome him into the world and make sure he's healthy. That's the number one thing right now, got it?"

Still in shock from the news about Ashland, I said, "Yes, that's the number one thing. Ashland's baby. Oh God, please protect him. Momma!"

"Yes, darling."

"I know you wanted to be in here, but I need you praying for Ashland. Let Detra Ann stay with me, and you go pray. When Rachel gets here, get her praying too. Please, Momma. Pray your very hardest!" I cried as the sweat poured off my forehead.

"What's the air on?" Detra Ann asked the nurse. Without waiting she checked the room thermostat and immediately dropped it. It didn't do any good because just then the lights went out. In the momentary silence I could hear the winds rattling the windows of the hospital like moaning ghosts demanding to be let in.

"I've had enough of ghosts! You hear me? Enough!"

Dr. Gary stared at me. "Carrie Jo, are you with me? Nurse, check her IV bag. I did not order anything that would make her hallucinate."

Detra Ann assured him I was fine, that I was just worried about Ashland, and then the labor began in earnest. "Okay, let's check. Yes, fully dilated. That was fast once you got started. That's a good thing. Some people have the worst time opening up. Let's see...oh yes, I see a little head already. Now it's important that you push when I tell you to push, okay. Are you in pain?"

"No pain, just a lot of pressure. Can I push yet?"

"Let me get in position. Okay, let's push."

I sat up and held my knees, pushing with all my might. *This isn't right. This shouldn't be happening. Not without my husband. Ashland, I love you. Where are you!*

I need you right now! Two hours later Ashland returned with my overnight bag. He and baby AJ would stay home until it was time to release Deidre. She'd been in and out of consciousness but hadn't said much beyond "I'm okay" and "I love you, Carrie Jo."

Ashland hugged me and convinced me to grab a bite to eat in the cafeteria. "She'll be up for a visit once the medication wears off, and I don't want to go home wondering if you ate today. I can just about bet you skipped lunch."

"How did you know?" I whispered guiltily as we walked out the door.

"First full day on a new house? It's kind of a no-brainer."

There wasn't much left in the Springhill Memorial Hospital cafeteria, so I opted for a cup of the least offensive-looking soup and a half sandwich and sweet iced tea. Ashland grabbed an apple, and we headed to a quiet corner near the atrium. We didn't talk for a long while. I moved various vegetables around in the broth with my plastic spoon and removed the cling wrap from my club sandwich. I didn't feel much like eating.

"You think it could be possible? Could I have a brother?"

He squeezed my hand and kissed my forehead. "If you have a brother, we'll find him. But remember what the nurse said. It's not unusual for people to think crazy things when they have had a head injury like hers."

"That's not exactly what she said."

"Have you ever heard of Chance Jardine?"

"Never. Not once. But then again, I don't even know my father's name. Granted I haven't asked in the past year, but she's never been very forthcoming about her past. I used to make up stories about him when I was a kid. I got tired of the other kids asking."

"What kind of stories?"

"You name it. I told my fourth grade teacher that he played in the NFL."

"I like the idea of making up a dad story. I wish I could have gotten away with something like that. But then I was never that creative, and everyone in Mobile knew my father. And most people didn't like him." He munched on his apple absently.

"That's the thing. I would like to know something—anything—about him. If he was an awful person, I would want to know about it. As it stands now, I know he had green eyes like mine because my mother's eyes are brown. I don't know squat."

He didn't say anything else. What could he say that would make me feel better? I ate a few bites of the sandwich, tried the soup and declared myself full. "Ready to go back?" After depositing the trash in the can, we took the elevator back upstairs.

"Almost forgot. Rachel left some papers at the house. Said they had to be signed and faxed first thing in the morning. You forgot them today. She said she would have waited, but as there was no fax machine at Idlewood, she figured you'd need to send them from the office or home. I told her where you were and what was up. Said she'd cover for you if you needed her to."

"Ugh, I forgot about those. Yeah, I'll sign them. Would you mind taking them back and sending them for me? She's right. They are time-sensitive documents."

"I think I can handle that."

"No word from Detra Ann?" I asked him cautiously. I missed her. It was weird having a crisis without her blond head all up in the middle of it.

"Nothing, but I know she's still in town. I've seen her car at her mother's house."

"I have a big mouth," I said as we stepped off the world's slowest elevator.

"Maybe, but you have a big heart. She'll come around. I promise."

I threw my arms around him and buried my face in his shirt. He smelled like fabric softener and baby lotion and expensive cologne. I breathed him in and kissed his neck once. "You better go." I glanced at my watch. "Can you believe it's eight o'clock already? AJ is probably wailing for his bath. I'll sign the Idlewood papers and let you go take care of our rug rat."

"I think I can handle that too," he said with a smile.

"I know you can." I unzipped the bag and pulled out the manila envelope. I flipped through the stack of familiar papers—requisition forms that Mr. Taylor's office required, a few special order forms from Zagfield in Atlanta related to the lights in the house and a few other miscellaneous papers that required my signature.

Underneath the stack to be signed was a paper clipped bundle of articles printed from various webpages. In Rachel's neat handwriting, the sticky note on top read: "For Carrie Jo."

"I think that's all that needed to be signed. I'll text you later when she wakes up. Unless it's late."

"Knowing our son, I'll be up anyway. I love you, Carrie Jo."

"Love you, too," I whispered as he walked out with the papers. I glanced at my mother, who hadn't moved. There was a Naugahyde recliner in the corner. That would be my bed for the night. I turned the main light off and flipped on the track light over the chair. Let her rest while she could. I pulled out some socks from the overnight bag. Ashland was so thoughtful to remember the small things. I had perpetually cold feet, and it was cold in here. I pulled my hair into a ponytail and leaned back to read what Rachel sent me. On each page she'd put sticky notes pointing out different things.

I was kind of familiar with what I was reading, but it hadn't been put together so succinctly before. To be honest, I wasn't sure why she was sharing all this with me: articles about the missing children, the interview with Beatrice Overton, the photos of apparitions that were supposedly the ghosts of Idlewood. When I took this job I hadn't believed there would be anything like this to consider, and having heard Desmond Taylor's warning I knew I shouldn't encourage Rachel in her curiosity to get to the bottom of this. True, I had dreamed about the children, and I was curious too, but I'd dreamed about places and people before. That didn't always mean I had to do something about it. Momma stirred a little on the bed and moaned in her sleep as if she were having a bad dream. I'd even dreamed about her when I was little. When she was in the middle of her breakdown or whatever it was when I was a child, I could see her dreams. They were dark, knotted and often full of snakes and other creepy things. I'd done my dead level best to avoid napping with my mom from then on.

I wondered what it would be like now, now that she was taking her medication and getting the help she needed. And if I did dream with her, would I find the answer to the question I wanted to uncover most right now? Who was Chance Jardine? That was something to consider. Maybe I would do that tonight. She couldn't object because she'd be out of it. But then again, we were at a new level in our relationship. We'd worked to repair some trust between us, and I wouldn't be the one to break it.

But who was Chance Jardine?

I sighed and continued to flip through the pages as quietly as possible. I found a handwritten note from Rachel. *Thought you should see these. Let me know what you think.* She'd found a photograph of a family oil painting, but I didn't need to read the inscription to know who they were. This was the Ferguson family, in happier days, presumably before Percy's marriage to Aubrey. I couldn't help but stare at the face of the youngest one, Trinket. She seemed so vulnerable. Her eyes were so large compared to the rest of her, and they were like two smudges of sadness. They pleaded with me. I could almost hear her voice.

Find her.

Find me.

Help us.

Chapter Thirteen—Trinket

I screamed as Bridget chased me down the garden path. She held one of her vicious-looking hatpins in her hand, and her intentions were clear. She thrust it at me, and I felt the evil tip poke my flesh. My scrawny legs pumped faster underneath my flimsy dress as I managed to race ahead of her, and I scrambled down the steps of the sunken garden. Today's weapon was the prettiest one in her collection, my favorite, the one with the butterfly wings. The enamel wings were lovely, but make no mistake, this was a tool of torture. My sister enjoyed piercing me to make me bleed. How I howled and screamed, but she was merciless in her pursuit of blood, which had become much more frequent a demand of late.

Especially since the death of our Golden Sister, Tallulah. She would never have approved of such vicious blood-letting.

But Bridget needed the blood, she explained, to summon the fairies. They loved the taste of innocent blood—and she needed the fairies' power to resurrect Tallulah. At night, when the house was dark and quiet, she would remind me that Tallulah would linger in purgatory for all eternity and needed freedom. Her whispers filled my heart with fear and deep sadness. The kind my heart had never experienced before, even as familiar as I was with sadness.

I dipped behind a short wall. I had to stop and try to catch my breath. Then she found me. Bridget stood over me, her pin raised high above her head like I was a fish ready to be spiked and she the fisherman. I screamed as tears streamed down my face. I'd quit begging for mercy. She wasn't listening.

"Why all the fuss, Trinket? I am *not* going to kill you. I want to bring our sister back. Why won't you help? You are so selfish! Always so selfish! Give me some of your sweet blood!"

"Use your own blood!" I screamed defiantly.

"It must be innocent, sister. I won't kill you—now be still."

With that meager hope, the hope that she would not kill me, I gave up. I let my body sag and prepared for the piercing blow. I was crying so hard my chest was shuddering. I found it hard to breathe.

Even the oversize bow on the top of my head sagged. How I hated Mother for insisting that I wear these. If I survived this involuntary offering, I vowed to myself that I would never wear another one again. What could Mother do to me that was worse than what Bridget, the Queen of the Fairies, was about to rain down upon me? My hand went up defensively, but the blow never came.

I hid behind my raised arm and decided to beg for mercy one last time. "Bridget! No! Don't do this! Tallulah wouldn't let you! Tallulah!"

Maybe my words struck her heart, for Bridget stepped back. Her feet dragged on the dirt floor as if she were frozen to the spot and could move them only with the greatest of personal force. "Sss...." was the only sound she made as her body shook. She sounded as if the air had been let out of her, squeezed out by an invisible hand. She dropped the long, slender pin; it fell in front of me, and like a madwoman I grabbed it before she could retrieve it.

I watched Bridget turn to run from the unseen interloper, and that moment felt like an eternity. Her arms were akimbo like a heathen dancer who worshiped around a fire. My sister's thick brown hair swirled about her shocked pale face, kept in place only by the wreath of flowers upon her head. She left me alone to fight whatever she feared so completely. I leaned against the damp block wall in the sunken garden to collect my wits. Still clutching the hatpin, as it was my only defense, I peeked out from around the corner of the blocks.

In an instant I recognized her.

Tallulah!

I leaned back with a gasp, still unable to breathe. Who or what could that be? Yet the image of her—her once cheerful yellow gown, the white skin of her arms, her blond hair—was ingrained in my mind. I had to be mistaken. "Bridget!" I whispered through hot tears. This had to be a trick! A cruel trick of the fairies. Yes, that had to be it. Or the fear of my sister had made me lose my mental faculties. I was very close to losing my bladder now.

Holding the butterfly-topped pin in my hands like a sword, I swung around the corner again, ready to face the hideous doppelganger. But the thing had vanished. In its place, a thick green field of grass filled with yellow butterflies mocking me as they fluttered about carelessly. I would never love a butterfly again.

I walked home, and it seemed much farther than I remembered. I didn't realize how far I'd run. I was tired now and hungry. My stomach rumbled its complaint. I went to the kitchen house, and Mr. Lofton gave me a sweet roll. At least there was one kind soul in this place. And Mrs. Potts, she was another kind one, although she was nowhere near as kind as Mr. Lofton. He was my favorite. And not just because he gave me baked treats whenever I asked for them.

I didn't come into the main house but entered through the servants' quarters and tiptoed up the stairs. A neat trick in my noisy new shoes. I hated shoes and would have much preferred wearing soft slippers every day. I heard someone weeping, but someone was always weeping now that Tallulah had died. And I was often among them. I had no more tears at this present moment, however, and I felt tremendous guilt over that. My sister had been dead for less than a month, and I couldn't muster up one more tear, although my heart hurt so much at times I was sure it must be bleeding. Did hearts bleed? I stuffed the remaining bit of my treat into my mouth and dug in my pocket with my sticky hand. Yes, I still had the pin. I held my breath as I passed the door of the bedroom I shared with Bridget. She watched me approach, and I closed it against me. No bother to me. I would not stay with her again. I would sleep in the nursery; I was still a child, after all. And nobody would miss me.

"No, I will not be quiet! You have no right to be rifling through her things. If you want dresses or purses or hats, I will buy them for you, but stay out of here."

"What is wrong with you? I was only putting her things away! I do not want your sister's clothing! This is the way things are done, Percy. When someone dies, you put their things away." She was trying to calm him, but it wasn't working. I could have told her she was wasting her time. "It helps preserve the things that were the most precious to the deceased, and it gives the grieving some relief. I would think you would want to give your mother some relief. She spends all her time crying over your sister. Have you no heart, Percy?"

I peeked through the crack in the doorway and saw that Percy towered above her. I knew that look. He wanted to push her down, just as he used to do to Michael when Michael was cruel to me or, God forbid, cruel to Tallulah. He would push him down and stand over him in a threatening way until Michael agreed to behave. But he could not push Aubrey down. She was his wife, and husbands did not do such things to their wives.

In a stilted voice he said, "I do not care what other people do. I do not want her things touched or plundered through. Leave it be, Aubrey."

"Even in death you love her more!" she began but soon hushed her mouth.

"Be careful what you say to me, Mrs. Ferguson." She opened and closed her mouth like one of the goldfish in the pond and looked away. Percy stormed out of the room and moved so quickly that he nearly tripped over me. "You shouldn't be here, Dot."

"I know," I said, unafraid of my brother. He would never push me down. "Look!" I waved the pin at him. "Look what I took from Bridget." I showed him the pin in an attempt to take his mind off his adult troubles. He waved me away, uninterested.

"Not now." He stomped down the hall and then down the stairs. I turned my attention back to the door. Aubrey was folding something. A piece of paper. So that was what she was after. She lit a match and crumpled the paper, tossing it in the fireplace. I pushed on the door to get a better look, but it squeaked loudly and betrayed my position.

"Percy?" she called.

I pushed the door open, anxious to see what exactly she planned to do with the paper she seemed so concerned about burning. I didn't answer her but walked into Tallulah's room confidently and smiled at her as she froze. The match extinguished in her fingers, but she did not blow it out. She sat up nervously and fussed with her skirts. Then offense crept over her plain face. "How long have you been spying on Percy and me and lurking outside our door? That is very rude, Dot. Do not spy on married couples."

"Only Percy calls me Dot. You may call me Trinket." I felt the sharp pin in my pocket. It gave me confidence. Surely that feeling was some kind of fairy magic.

"Very well—Trinket. Let me be perfectly clear. It is very rude to go about spying on married people. You might see something you cannot unsee."

"I shall remember that. You may go now, Aubrey. This is my room."

"No, it isn't. This room belongs to your dead sister." I hated seeing the smirk on her face. She was plain, very plain. Bridget secretly called her "horse face" behind her back. I tried not to giggle about it. I decided right then and there I would fix this problem. I'd been bullied enough today. It was time to do some bullying of my own.

"She will share it with me." I looked around as if I could see Tallulah right now. I took a step toward Aubrey, my eyes fixed on her face. "And lost souls lurk at Idlewood. They always have, and now there is one more," I lied. My skin crept up in goose bumps as I spoke, as if by saying these things I did indeed have the power to make them true. "Tallulah will not like you being here in our room. She likes her privacy."

"What foolishness is this? Something your sister Bridget cooked up? Honestly, this house is a madhouse. Between your squalling mother, leering brother and fairy-crazed sister, it is a wonder you aren't all in the sanitarium."

I did not back down despite the intended offense. She was a hateful girl, and she did not like me now that I had caught her doing something criminal. Yet she had forgotten about the paper, and I wanted it that way.

"Oh, it is true. The spirits stir today, Aubrey." I showed her my pin. I even pricked my own finger with it in front of her and bit my lip so I wouldn't cry out. I let the blood droplets hit the floor. How angry Bridget would have been to see my precious blood gone to waste. "My sister, Tallulah, was in the garden just a few minutes ago. I saw her. Why would she linger here if not for revenge? I wonder if there is something she forgot to do. Something left undone? Perhaps she wants to tell us a secret. Yes, that's probably it!"

Aubrey smirked again. "I don't think we need to guess why she would be here. She is *damned*. Anyone who takes her own life is *damned*. Dead and damned. Now stop this childish talk."

I took another step toward her, the pin still in my hand. I felt rage rising up inside me, rage that she would speak so ill of my dead Golden Sister. Although I did not know why, I knew that Aubrey hated Tallulah, even in death.

"No. She will never rest."

And yet another step. Now I was between her and the fireplace. She remembered and wanted to retrieve the paper. I could see her face become even more pinched. She made a half step toward the crumpled ball, but I stamped my foot like an angry horse. She tried again, and I stamped again and waved the pin like a wand. I put myself between the paper and her, the pin in my hand. It was like I was Bridget now. Mad and ready to pierce flesh. How had this happened?

She scowled at me and left Tallulah's room. No. Now it was my room. I would insist on it. When the wooden door closed behind me, I threw the pin in the small stack of firewood and retrieved the unlit paper. I knew right away it was a letter. A letter to Tallulah from Aubrey.

I sat on the floor and read it, and then read it again.

Dear Sister, Our Tallulah,

Although it is very kind of you to greet us at every station with a letter, I must ask that you refrain from doing so further. Your letters, though sweet and entertaining in the beginning, have become a source of discomfort to your brother, especially in light of the knowledge that you have chosen to refuse marriage to Richard Chestnut, a respectable man in our county who wants to make you lady of your own house. How angry Percy became when he heard of your truculent attitude and your refusal to provide him this happiness! Upon hearing the news of your miserable behavior, it took all my wits to keep him from returning home to compel you to behave with proper decorum. Even your father is nearing wit's end.

It is time to grow up, sister. Time to leave childhood things and affections behind.

Now please, dear Tallulah, refrain from upsetting your brother further with your notes. For we know what you intend, and it displeases us greatly. Only write us to tell us that you will indeed marry Mr. Richard Chestnut, who is also my own cousin and tells me he thinks of nothing but becoming your bridegroom. I can vouch that he is an honorable man who will shower you with affection.

Put your brother's mind at ease. Write to say that you will no longer reside at Idlewood with us, that you have found a new place with Mr. Chestnut at Laurie House. This and only this is what I will convey to him, sister. If you cannot obey your father, brother and all of those who advise you, then please do not write to us again. We will speak of this matter no more until our return.

We will return to Mobile at the completion of our Honeymoon sometime within the next month. Please see that my china and other items are installed safely in their proper places. These generous gifts from your brother deserve a place of honor in our home at Idlewood.

With Disappointment and Sadness,

Mrs. Aubrey Ferguson

Again, my child's mind did not understand the inner workings of adulthood, but even I knew this was not a kind letter from a loving "sister." Certainly not one that Tallulah would have enjoyed receiving. So why was Aubrey trying to burn it unless she wanted to prevent Percy from reading it? Then and there I pledged to myself and the ghost of my sister that I would see that he did read it! Percy would know the truth!

I shook with the knowledge that filled my mind.

Tallulah had done the evil deed when she was out of her mind! It had been Aubrey who had tricked Tallulah! Percy would never have written such a letter nor sanctioned Aubrey to do so! Wicked girl, indeed!

Now what should I do? No doubt Aubrey would be back for her letter. I couldn't leave it here. I'd have to put it somewhere safe. Very safe. Where nobody could find it and burn it.

Where magic would protect it.

Forever.

***

Suddenly the sound of crying broke into my dream. It was my mother's voice that woke me. I slung back the thin sheet I'd covered up with and walked to her hospital bed quietly. She was whispering, whispering something.

Percy… such a letter…Wicked girl, indeed!

I couldn't explain it, and I had not expected it, but the truth was pretty plain. My mother was a dream catcher. Whether she could dream walk on her own or only with someone else, she had heard and seen my dream. I had the proof now. No more wondering where I got the gift from.

How long had this been going on?

Oh, Momma! What else haven't you told me?

Chapter Fourteen—Detra Ann

I'd had three days of serious depression—but no drinking so far. That was a miracle. I slipped out of my mother's house; I'd been staying in her guest room and ignoring her attempts to come and chat with me. I didn't want to see her gloat. I knew she'd always had her doubts about Henri and wouldn't hold back now, but there was more to it than she knew. And I wasn't up for the same old arguments we'd had a million times before.

I'd bought the bottle on the way here and put it in the center of the table. For three days, I walked by it and stared at it. Eventually, I opened it. But I couldn't bring myself to drink it. I wanted to. I wanted to forget Henri and even T.D. and everything else.

But I didn't want to forget Lenore, who gave her life for me.

I didn't want to forget Aleezabeth.

I didn't want to forget who Harry and I had been.

Instead, I'd go find Aleezabeth. And then whatever happened, happened. I didn't know how, but my destiny was all tangled up with a dead girl's, and I had to figure out how to untangle it. Nothing was ever easy, was it?

I drove to New Orleans and checked into Hotel Monteleone. It was a lovely old hotel, and I'd been here before while in college. One day, Henri and I would come here and celebrate our marriage with a lengthy honeymoon. That first night in New Orleans, I ate a good meal, the first one in days, and went back to my room. I began making phone calls and arranged a meeting with a detective that my cousin Alcide had recommended.

His name was Brendan Bennett; he was a lifelong resident of the Dumont area and was familiar with my case. He gave me his price, and I agreed to it and told him I expected answers soon. We were meeting for coffee in the morning. So why did I pick this guy over everyone else? Because he hadn't lied to me. Not once. I liked that. He didn't promise me anything, but he was confident and knew how to proceed.

I reread the very lengthy texts Carrie Jo sent me. I wasn't angry with her. I just wanted to do this alone. This would be my wedding gift to Harry. *I* would be the one to set him free. That's what you did for the people you loved. And I knew he loved me. I didn't agree that we must wait to marry, but I wasn't going to belabor the point any longer with him.

I was going to get it done, one way or another. I was going back to Mobile with the Aleezabeth mystery solved. No matter how long it took. No matter what it cost me. I would make this happen. I scanned the texts from Carrie Jo for information again. Apparently Ashland had seen Aleezabeth on a regular basis. *Thanks for telling us, buddy.* And to make matters more complicated, according to Ashland, Aleezabeth passed on some valuable information. She had been with a man with a mustache who played the saxophone when she disappeared. I knew that description fit Harry's father. If Harry believed Ashland, he would suspect his father. No love lost between those two. We didn't even know if he was alive or dead, and when I'd once mentioned finding him, Harry had lost it. There'd been no convincing him. I suspected all that would change now.

I'd know more tomorrow. In the meantime I crawled in the bed and flipped through the photos on my phone. My favorite was about halfway into the pictures from the night Harry had surprised me with the ring. He'd been so sweet, and thousands of pairs of eyes had been on me. Of course, my mother thought it was hokey proposing on a Jumbotron, but I loved it. If we could have gotten married right then, I would have done it. Yeah, this was kind of my fault. He'd begged me to run off to Vegas with him, but I'd insisted on a church wedding. And when that fell through (thanks to good old Mom), I'd come up with the brilliant idea of getting married at Seven Sisters. It seemed right at the time.

Now I realized that I'd made a mistake. I shouldn't have insisted that we wait—who knew if we'd make it to the altar at all now? New Orleans was a noisy place, even at night, but I liked the noise. It let me know that even though Death came for me once, I'd escaped it. I had a life ahead of me. A good life with the man I loved. I couldn't go another night without texting him, so I did just that.

In New Orleans. I'm okay. I'll call soon.

Immediately I got a text back.

Be safe. I'm here. I love you.

I answered with a smiley face and fell asleep. I felt like I had just closed my eyes when I woke to the sound of someone knocking politely on the door. I wasn't expecting anyone, but I did glance at the clock. It was seven a.m. right on the dot. "Who is it?" I asked cautiously. New Orleans wasn't the place to be swinging open doors without asking questions first.

"Room service, ma'am. I have breakfast with coffee."

I shoved my wild hair away from my face, pulled on a t-shirt and a pair of shorts, pattered to the door and peeked out the peephole. Definitely a tray and a pot of steaming coffee. A woman in a white coat. Looked legit, but she must have had the wrong room.

I opened the door and said, "That smells wonderful, but I didn't order any breakfast." I crossed my arms and leaned against the doorframe. No sense in being hard on the woman. She was just trying to do her job. Besides, if there was more where that came from, I was definitely interested. The young woman pulled a card from the tray and stared at the door number.

"417. That's right. Breakfast for one for Detra Ann Dowd, courtesy of Henri Devecheaux. Oh, and the flowers are from him too."

"What?" A goofy smile spread across my face.

"Yes, ma'am. Would you like me to set that up for you on the balcony?"

"Sure." I let her in, and she quickly set up the small table and pulled out a chair.

"Thank you so much."

"You are welcome." She smiled down with her hand on the silver lid. With a polite flourish, she removed the lid. I nearly cried—it was a plate of hot beignets and a cup of fresh fruit. My absolute favorite breakfast. She poured me a cup of black coffee and laid a linen napkin in my lap. "When you're finished, just set the tray outside. I'll be back for it in a bit. Enjoy your breakfast."

"Thank you again. I didn't catch your name."

"It's Mitch. Like Margaret Mitchell, not Michelle."

"Mom a fan of Scarlett O'Hara's?"

"You don't know the half of it. My sister's name is Melanie."

"Well, at least you didn't get stuck with Scarlett."

She rolled up her sleeve and showed me a bright tattoo that read: Scarlett Mitchell Jones. It made me smile.

"Nice to meet you, Mitch. Thanks again."

With a polite smile, Mitch left me to cry in my beignets alone.

Chapter Fifteen—Rachel

Gran placed tick marks on her Disney calendar with a fat-barreled red Sharpie. She had something planned in T-minus seven days, and although she was very hush-hush about it, she seemed very excited. This would be her sixty-fifth birthday, and she was bound and determined to do something she'd never done before. Nobody knew what the something was, but I was pretty sure it involved my old room. It was a puzzle, and when she got ready to tell me about it, I'd know. I couldn't believe it was March already.

Things had "quieted down" at Idlewood, but I had a sneaking suspicion it had a lot to do with the number of people coming in and out of there. After the mold issue got resolved we moved on to Sheetrock, woodwork and painting on the construction side. On the historical side, we worked with our Adept software to create a catalog of items with notes about placement, requisition and a thousand other things. Sadly, I spent a lot of time at the office now since Mr. Taylor placed a heavy emphasis on the paperwork side of things. He was very much a numbers kind of guy. At least his wife was a sweet person. But I was at the house a couple of times a week, and not just to see Angus. Whenever I went to Idlewood I still felt eyes watching me; I heard the occasional whisper of *Rachel Kowalski* and heard the sound of tiny feet running in the attic above me from time to time whenever I walked around the second floor.

Carrie Jo mentioned that she'd dreamed about the house a few times, but with the drama unfolding with her best friend and her mother, she hadn't given me any details about what it was that she saw.

"Are you sure he has to come by tonight? What if I wanted to walk around in my underwear?"

"Gran, I don't understand you. I *know* you don't like him. Tell me why." I slapped my hand on the counter and put the other one on my hip. She gave me a shrug and put the Sharpie back in its caddy. "Why are you being so evasive?" When I could see she wasn't going to tell me anything else, I put the finishing touches on my Chicken Doritos casserole and slid it in the oven. Forty minutes of baking time, and then it was ooey-gooey chicken heaven. Hopefully Angus appreciated a good casserole because this was my go-to recipe. Well, the only one I felt comfortable offering to anyone I liked.

My mother was off tonight, so this worked out perfectly. I wanted her to meet him. Surely she'd like him. I couldn't figure out Gran.

"He's going to get you into trouble," Gran said matter-of-factly as she poured herself a glass of peach iced tea.

I laughed nervously. "Gran, we haven't even kissed yet. I hardly think he's going to get me in trouble."

"Not that kind of trouble, Miss Smarty Pants." The doorbell rang, and I hugged her playfully.

"I'll be fine. Now put on a happy face and trust me." I handed her my apron and practically bounced to the front door. As I passed my apartment door, I quickly closed it. I wasn't ready to invite Angus into my room yet, and even after the move I hadn't put everything away. Nope, I wasn't rushing this relationship, not like I did with Chip. I regretted that misstep big time. Strangely enough I knew that Angus would have liked Chip, but I wasn't sure that the feeling would have been mutual. Chip hated all things supernatural, and Angus had a real love for them. In fact, he was an amateur ghost hunter as well as an electrical genius. That thrilled me down to my socks.

Angus had finally come clean with me about his first visit to Idlewood. He worked for the electrical contractor we hired, but he'd only stopped by that day to take a peek at the house. Apparently the reason he left without saying goodbye was because someone shoved him so hard it took the wind out of him. An invisible someone. He'd been busy digging in his truck for a tool when wham! It hit him on the back and launched him halfway into the van. When he could finally get up, he left. Not very chivalrous, I pointed out, but he apologized for his abrupt departure. And I accepted it. Gran called me naïve, but so what? I *did* believe him.

If Detra Ann were back from New Orleans, I'd have asked her for her opinion. But as it stood now, I had no reason not to trust him.

Despite the fact he'd come to the house under false premises and ran like a scared dog at the first sign of trouble.

"Howdy!" I said, welcoming him into the house. He'd been here at least a dozen times before, and as always he wiped his shoes and hung up his jacket politely. I could hear Gran's bedroom door shut, but I smiled through it.

Mom walked in the living room with her nose in a paperback. I had a pretty mother, very pretty. She was taller than me by three inches and had silky black hair that she liked to pull back in a barrette. Tonight she wore some "mom clothes," thankfully, and she greeted Angus like he was my high school sweetheart.

"Nice to meet you Angus. Dinner smells wonderful, Rachel. Can I get you guys something to drink?" I liked my mother. I knew not everyone could say that about their mothers, but she was a nice lady. Even if she was a bit distant at times. She worked hard and treated me well … I had nothing to complain about. I wished she'd get out more, but hey, who was I to judge? She did love cuddling up with her Harlequins. In fact, for her birthday I'd loaded her up with a box of them I'd found in great condition at the Goodwill.

"So what's that one called, Mom?"

"Torn Asunder in the Highlands," she said with a big grin. "Oh my. I hope that's not offensive."

"Um…" Angus rubbed his ginger eyebrow and grinned. "No, but it doesn't sound too romantic to me."

With that we sat on Gran's plaid sofas and talked about what it was like growing up in Scotland. Angus and my mother were both exceedingly polite. It was weird. Ten minutes before supper was ready, Gran came down, thankfully not in her underwear.

"Rachel? Is supper ready yet? I've got to take my medicine, and I need to eat soon."

"What?" I said laughingly.

"Would you mind getting me something to drink?"

"Uh, sure, Gran. Where is your glass?" I sure didn't want to leave Angus alone with my grandmother, but I couldn't tell her no.

"Left it upstairs."

"Okay," I said cautiously. I gave Angus a shrug as I left the room. He didn't seem to notice there was a thing wrong. When it came to detecting uncomfortable situations, he wasn't that good at it. I hoped he was a better ghost detective.

Which was another reason why he came by tonight. We hadn't told a soul, and I knew it was kind of unethical, but we were going to Idlewood after dinner. He wanted to see a ghost, and I knew there was at least one there. But then, so did he, didn't he? I already had my backpack ready to go complete with a flashlight, walkie-talkies, a camera and power bars. I liked to eat when I got nervous. And I sure as heck didn't plan on staying all night. I found Gran's glass and walked back toward the stairs when I noticed that the door to my old bedroom stood open. In the window a candle burned. And not a scented one, just a short stub of a dusty white candle and an even dustier glass holder. I didn't recognize either of them, but that meant nothing. Gran went through a stage where she was burning candles for everything. Healing, prosperity, breaking curses—you name it. This must have been the remnants of one of those. Still, it was odd because there was nothing else in here, just the burning candle. Who was the candle for? How many times had she scolded me for leaving candles burning in the house when no one was home? I walked over to it and blew it out. She must have forgotten about it. What was up with her lately?

The lack of light left the bare room dark as the night outside. There was faint light from the hallway, but it was a light from the street that grabbed my attention. Someone was there and looking up at the house. It was a child. A little girl stood under the streetlight, her face darkened by the large oak that stood nearby. She didn't belong. I knew that. She didn't belong! She didn't belong on the street, and she didn't belong in this world. She stepped out of the darkness and continued to stare up at me. I could see her oversize bow on her head and her long, torn dress with the ribbons in the back. She had no socks or shoes on. I tapped the window to let her know I saw her, and then I heard the voice in my ear.

Rachel Kowalski…

I stared out from the second-story window and forgot about the glass I was holding in my hand. It crashed to the ground and shattered into pieces. Luckily for me, I didn't cut myself. "Oh heck!" I squatted down and started picking up the pieces. By the time I was done, she was gone.

I walked down the carpeted stairs as discreetly as possible so I could snoop and hear what was going on in there. I heard my mother's pretend-shocked voice, "Mom…" I refilled the glass and brought it to Gran, who was now leaning back in her recliner with a satisfied smile on her face. For the first time ever, Angus appeared uncomfortable, even disheveled.

"Here you go, Gran. Um, Angus? Will you come help me set the table?"

"Hey! We'll all help. Well, except you, Sabrina. You wait on people all the time. I can help, though." Everything went smoothly after that, except Angus. He looked nervous, and I was dying to ask him what happened or what inappropriate thing my grandmother said to him. Dinner went awkwardly. Nobody much spoke, but at least Mom put her book to the side long enough to eat. Gran offered to do the dishes, and we'd planned that I was going to say we were going for a walk, grab my backpack and meet him in the car.

"You know, I just remembered I have to do something for my boss. It sounds stupid, I know, but I have to go." He was by the front door, putting on his shoes and sliding on his jacket. "Rain check on the rest of the evening?"

"Rain check? What? I thought we were going to…"

"I can't, Rachel. I'll make it up to you. I promise." My mother passed by and he said, "Goodnight, Sabrina." To me he said sadly, "Tell your Gran goodnight too."

Mom gave a pleasant goodnight and walked into her room with her book and her nightly glass of wine. Gran was busy in the kitchen and didn't answer him. I touched his arm and whispered, "Did my grandmother say something or offend you somehow? She doesn't mean it; I swear she's not crazy. And I saw something. Right here—right upstairs! Can you believe that? Surely you aren't going to pass up this opportunity to see…" I half-joked.

"No. Nothing like that. I'll text you later. Night, Rachel." He squeezed my hand and walked out the door, leaving me to stare after him. What the heck just happened? How could I like a guy who let my Gran run him off? And why would she do that? I watched Angus' truck pull out and rolled my eyes. I'd just seen the little ghost girl from Idlewood—I was pretty sure it was her, anyway—and my so-called detective partner bailed on me. Whatever, dude. I closed the door and went to my room. Flopping on the bed, I stared at my backpack. I didn't need his help. I'd do my own investigation. I kind of had to now. She'd showed up at my house! What was I supposed to do?

I changed clothing, opting for comfortable jeans, a hoodie sweatshirt and my favorite Converse tennis shoes. I grabbed my backpack and car keys, then left the house without saying goodbye. I wouldn't be gone long, and quite frankly I wasn't in the mood to chat with my family.

It was a ten-minute drive from my house in midtown Mobile to the house on Carlen Street. I made the turn off the street and climbed the steep driveway. As I rounded the hill Idlewood rose like an imposing old castle looming over the surrounding countryside. No lights were on, not even a porch light. It was springtime in Mobile, so naturally there was plenty of fog to make the place look even more gloomy and foreboding. I put the car in park and turned it off.

Okay, why am I doing this? What did I hope to achieve by exploring Idlewood at night? I glanced at my watch. It was only ten o'clock. Not that late, right? And it was Friday, so I could hear the sounds of life rising up from the surrounding streets. I heard jazz playing from a local club; nearby Dauphin Street was bustling with crowds who liked visiting the microbreweries, dance clubs and a host of other venues. But here, right here, all that fell away.

Then I saw her, the same small girl who'd stood beneath the streetlight outside my house earlier. Her damp hair hung in clumps around her face. She wore a dingy bow in her hair, and her dress had a dirt-stained ripped hem. All this I saw in a few seconds. She stood a few feet in front of my car, obscured by a patch of fog. And when the fog cleared, she was gone. My skin felt clammy, and I reached for my backpack. I knew why I was doing this. Because Trinket wanted me to. Yes, that was her name.

Suddenly I felt strangely calm, as if I were sliding into a pool of honey. All seemed right. I was doing the right thing. Even without Angus here. *I'm coming, Trinket!* I whispered into the darkness. Trinket, the missing child. One of the missing Ferguson children. As I walked toward the house, I could finally admit to myself that I'd been thinking about her for weeks. I'd spent hours scouring the internet, staring at her picture, pondering what might have happened to her. It was impossible to know, wasn't it? Trinket. I felt as if I would have known her sweet name even if I had not read it online. We were connected somehow. She was reaching out to me from the past. So helpless and lost. Trinket needed my help—to find her way back. She'd reached out to me.

Shoving my car keys in my pocket, I zipped up the backpack and walked on to the porch. I glanced toward the road. Nobody could see me from Carlen or Dauphin Street. Not a soul. I felt truly isolated now. The fog thickened so much that my car, which couldn't have been more than fifty feet behind me, was completely hidden from view. There was nothing now. Nothing but Idlewood. With a lump in my throat, I flipped on the light and reached for my keys. I had one, so there was no sense in sneaking in.

But I didn't need the shiny new key.

The front door slowly drifted open and revealed a massive black space. The darkness so permeated my view that I could barely discern the grandfather clock, an Austin-

Breem that I knew stood in the foyer. It had been an amazing find in the house, supposedly an original fixture, except that it didn't work despite the clockmaker's diligent efforts. I flashed my dim light over the 150-year-old clock and then around the room. I was alone. But not alone.

Out of the blackness above me, a voice whispered my name.

Rachel Kowalski...

Chapter Sixteen—Carrie Jo

I dried my hair with the towel as Ashland hung up the phone. From his relieved expression, I could tell that his conversation with Detra Ann went well. "She okay?"

"Yes, and she says to tell you she loves you. I think she's going to be okay. She swears she hasn't been drinking, and from the sound of it, she hasn't had the time to. She and the detective have spent the past few days interviewing witnesses."

"Has she called Henri?"

"Not yet. She says she doesn't want to talk to him until it's finished. All we can do is wait, I guess. Sure was nice of your mom to watch AJ for us tonight. I had a great time at the movies."

I stood between his legs and kissed him. "I hate lying to my mom." Ever since she got out of the hospital, she wanted nothing more than to spend time with baby AJ. So maybe we were just doing her a favor. Yeah, that was it.

"I know, but it wasn't really a lie. We did buy the tickets. Just didn't quite make it."

"I hope she doesn't ask for plot details." He laughed and the phone rang. We stared at each other. Nobody ever called us this late. Not even our friends.

"AJ!" I said as I ran to the phone in the hallway. "Hello?" Ashland was right behind me.

"Carrie Jo?"

"Yes?" I glanced at the caller ID. I didn't recognize the voice. Not right away. The call was coming from Rachel K's house. "This is CJ. Mrs. Kowalski?"

"Yes, this is Rachel's grandmother, Jan. I'm calling you because I think Rachel is going to do something stupid."

"What do you mean? Is she all right?"

"No, she's not. She's gone to Idlewood. By herself. And I can't explain it, but I have a very bad feeling about it."

"Don't say another word, Jan. We'll go check on her."

"Thank you. I'll meet you there." Jan hung up, and I raced to get dressed. Ashland threw on some clothes too, and we were downstairs and in the car in less than three minutes.

"What could she be doing? It's not like Rachel to get into séances and the like. She's not the thrill-seeking sort of person."

"I agree, babe. It's probably nothing. She might not even be there. Let's go check it out, and then we'll know what to do. You have your house keys?"

"Yep!" We sped down Government Street and were pulling into Idlewood in just a few minutes. It was kind of creepy out. Fog had rolled in off Mobile Bay and practically smothered the old house. "It's like the fog wants to hide the place."

"What?"

"Nothing. Just me being spooky. You see anything?"

"Just her car, and she's not in it." I could see the tension in Ashland's jaw. That didn't settle my nerves at all.

We pulled up beside Rachel's sporty car and stepped out cautiously. I practically ran to my husband and clutched his hand before the fog hid him from me completely. "So weird. Have you ever seen fog like this before?"

"I can't say that I have. Let's find out what's going on so we can go home. I don't see a single light on. The lights are working now, right?"

"Yeah, they've been working fine for weeks. The motion detector lights should have kicked on by now." We were at the foot of the stairs, and the front door stood wide open. I couldn't believe Rachel would leave it open like that. The fog was inside the house now. "Shoot," I whispered in frustration. Antique furniture and fog did not play well together.

"You have your phone? Just in case we need to call someone?" he asked as he peered into the house.

I snapped my fingers. "No, it's in the console of the car. Should I go back for it?"

"You stay here. I'll go." Before I could argue with him, he disappeared into the mist.

"Wait! Ashland!" I whispered after him, but I didn't know why I whispered. It wasn't like I didn't have permission to be here. He didn't answer me, and every second that passed by felt like an eternity. I hovered on the porch, unwilling to move inside without my husband's warm hand in mind. An unexpected sound changed my mind. A soft whispering, almost intelligible but not quite.

"Hello?" I whispered again as I stepped inside. My query was met with heavy footfalls crossing the floor above me. I spun around staring at the ceiling above me and heard a scream. I instantly knew it was Rachel. "Rachel!" I called up to her.

Anxious to check on my friend who even at this moment might be fighting off an intruder, I ran to the bottom of the stairs. "Rachel?"

The worst-case scenario played out in my head. Concerned about the house, Rachel came to check on Idlewood and make sure it was secure against this fog, and the intruder caught her off-guard. While I reasoned away, I heard a muffled scream. Then a glass broke and a horrible scraping sound took the place of the heavy footfalls.

Oh God. Oh God. Oh God.

I heard Rachel's panicked voice, and I couldn't linger any longer. I bounded up the stairs two by two when suddenly the front door slammed shut, shaking the house. I paused, but there was no turning back now. "Ashland?" I whispered once and then ran up the rest of the way. I stood on the top of the stairway confused by the sound of footfalls. Someone was approaching, stomping so loudly that the footsteps reverberated in my head, but I didn't see a single soul. I looked down at the floor. How could I be hearing footfalls like that? We'd had the runners installed this week, and all the hallways were carpeted now. Then I heard a child's voice whisper in my ear, "He's coming!"

I spun around, but there wasn't anyone in the hall with me. I ran to the nearest door and tried to open it, but it wouldn't budge. I shoved my shoulder into it. This wasn't a door with a lock. It should come open freely.

Please, oh please, oh please.

The door swung open, and I stumbled inside and closed it behind me. I was breathing so fast that I was practically hyperventilating. Where was Ashland?

"Carrie Jo?"

"Rachel?" I saw my friend's dark head appear over the side of the wooden basinet near the fireplace. I ran to her and put my arms around her neck. Then I moved her hair away from her wet face. "Oh, thank God. Are you okay? Who is that stomping?"

Her dark eyes were wide and damp with tears. She clutched my arm and whispered, "Look, over there. Do you see her?" She pointed her flashlight to the far corner of the room. A little girl sat on the floor, her thin arms wrapped around her knees. She wore an airy white dress, and her long brown hair covered her arms. I immediately knew who it was.

"Trinket," I said as the stomping got louder. Whoever was after Rachel or the ghost girl was getting closer. "Trinket," I whispered again. The child lifted her head, and for one nightmarish moment I thought I'd see something terrible, like a horrific wound or gaping black eyes. But it was only the face of a frightened little girl I'd seen in my dreams. I easily recognized the sad eyes and bow lips. She stared at us fearfully and raised her finger to her lips.

Help me.

The door swung open, and Rachel and I both screamed. I closed my eyes against the expected onslaught of violence, but when it didn't come, I peeked and watched as Trinket vanished. That was no specter standing in the doorway but my very much alive husband. Ashland flicked the light switch, and the room filled with warm light. There was no one here.

Only the living.

Chapter Seventeen—Carrie Jo

"Please, Carrie Jo," Rachel said. "You knew who she was. You have dreamed about her, haven't you?"

I nodded slowly. "Yes, I've seen her."

"Trinket came to the house, my house. She was outside under the light. She's reaching out for help. And I can't explain it, but I know she wanted me to come here. I hope you understand." Ashland opened a bottle of water and handed it to Rachel. He didn't say a word, but he was making Rachel and me nervous. He glanced over his shoulder occasionally, and once I thought I caught him ducking as if he were trying to dodge someone or something.

"It's not safe to be here. We need to go," he said in a deliberately even voice.

Rachel threw up her hands and said, "I know it's not safe. I've been chased all over the house tonight. But whatever this is, it has to happen tonight. I don't know what's required, but Trinket needs me. Please. We have to help her."

I looked at Ashland, who was definitely reluctant. Rachel sobbed again and stared down at the clump of tissues in her hand. We were sitting in the kitchen, and every light in the place was on. The stomping had ceased, but I could feel the shifting of the air. There was more to come. We weren't alone.

"You know, I thought I wanted this," Rachel whispered.

"What?" I asked, easing my chair closer and reaching for her hand.

"Our group of friends. Everyone has a supernatural gift, everyone but me. When I started seeing things here, feeling them so much more strongly, I thought that meant I belonged, that I had something to contribute. I've felt things before but never like this. But now, now I wish it would stop. Am I ever going to be able to turn these feelings off?"

"You were always a part of the group, Rachel. We love you. Yes, you will be able to turn the 'feelings' off. Just breathe. We will get through this. And you should know there is always a sense of urgency when you are dealing with the spirit world. Get used to that."

There was a knock at the back door, and we all jumped. "Okay, let's *all* breathe," Ashland said as he went to the door. Rachel's grandmother hurried in and immediately ran toward her with her arms outstretched. Rachel looked behind her grandmother, like she was looking for someone else, but there was nobody else coming. I saw disappointment cross her face before she smiled weakly at her grandmother.

"Girl! You gave me such a fright! Are you okay?"

"Yes, I'm fine, Gran. How did you know I was here? Angus tell you?"

"No, that boy didn't tell me anything. I just knew. I've been feeling the house pull at you for weeks now. I figured eventually you'd answer the call. Come on, let's go home. That fog is as thick as pea soup out there and not likely to dissipate anytime soon."

"What do you mean the house pulled at me? And *how* did you know?"

She wore a rain slicker even though it wasn't raining, a bright green one with a blue whale border at the bottom. With a shiver, from either the fog or something else, she said quietly but firmly, "We shouldn't speak of such things here. It isn't safe."

"I agree," Ashland said. "And no, it is not safe. Not in the least. Please, Carrie Jo, Rachel. Let's talk somewhere else. Our house is just around the corner. I'll make us a drink."

To my surprise, Rachel didn't put up a fight. Instead, relief washed over her. "A drink sounds good."

"Don't worry about the lights, Rach. I'll pop back in the morning and turn them off. Or someone will."

It must have been Providence that arranged for baby AJ to spend the night with my mom. I came home and turned on all the lights and some soothing music. Ashland poured whiskey over ice for Rachel and me. The younger woman took a few sips, then we sat back and waited for Jan to spill the beans. I had to admit I was just as curious as Rachel was. This time I didn't rush the conversation.

"A few weeks ago, Rachel, you asked me who you were. At the time I pretended not to understand the question, but I knew. I knew all along. You are a sensitive, and you come from a long line of Kowalski sensitives." To us all she said, "The Kowalskis are an ancient family. We can trace our Polish heritage back to the first millennium. Who else can do such a thing? And for as long as I can remember, there have always been mystics in our family tree. Don't let the name fool you, most of us were not strange pagans but Christian believers with supernatural powers. There are some people who say that ghosts are nothing more than demons, but we do not believe that. Yes, there are demons in the world and yes, they can trick you, but what I felt in that house was not a demon but ghosts. Many ghosts." She took her granddaughter's hands and said, "And there will be more because of you."

"Why have you never told me about this, Gran?"

"I am telling you now, Rachel. The time is right." To Ashland she said, "You are a seer of ghosts but beyond that, your skills are limited. Do you know why that is?"

"No, but I'm all ears." He was on his second drink now. His cheeks were flushed pink. I cuddled up in his arms on the couch.

"You see and can sometimes hear spirits because you were cursed, but you were lucky. You broke that curse. Now it is difficult to see what you saw easily before. Isn't that true?"

"Yes, it is true. How did you know?"

She didn't answer but tapped the side of her nose with her finger. Then she continued, "Your gift is fading. You have done nothing wrong, and you cannot do anything about it. Soon, you will renounce that gift. You will see something so horrible that will make you never want to see another ghost again. And when you pray for that gift to be taken, it will be gone in an instant. But beware, young man. You may come to regret that decision in years to come."

"And me?" I said, feeling brave for all of about two seconds.

"Your path is hidden from me. You have someone in your life who can tell you everything you need to know. You must ask her to tell you."

"She has amnesia. She doesn't remember quite a few things," I said honestly. And I had so many questions to ask her, like who the heck was Chance Jardine?

"When she remembers, you'll know all. Are you ready for that? You may wish you didn't, but you can't unring the bell. You can't unknow the knowing."

Rachel interrupted Jan's flow with a question. "That girl, the ghost girl, she wants me to help her, doesn't she? That's who's calling me?"

"There is more than one ghost in that house, and I wouldn't be surprised if you met them all at some time or another. This will be your first true test, Rachel. But as I told your friend, once Pandora's box is opened, there is nothing for it but to see the job through. Are you willing to do that?"

"I'm not sure," Rachel confessed. "If I understood it more, maybe so."

I cleared my throat. "I can tell you what I know. I think I know what's happening at the house. At least one part of it."

"Tell me, Carrie Jo. I have to know what to expect, what to do."

Ashland poured another drink. I watched him curiously as he kissed me on the top of my head. "Babe, I'm tired, and the baby will be back home in a couple of hours. I'm going to bed. I have to get some rest."

"Night, babe."

"Night, ladies." Ashland walked upstairs and left us alone.

Jan whispered to me, "Has he been propositioned by a woman recently?"

"Um, yes, actually. Right here in our home."

"Watch out for her. She's a witch. She's got her eye on him. She wants him and is willing to pay whatever price necessary to have him. I don't feel any curses on you—apparently you have some powerful protection and prayers covering you—but that doesn't mean she'll stop. If I were you, I'd get to church more often and burn some candles yourself, just to be sure. I burned a candle earlier this evening, a prayer candle, and for a while it kept the spirit away. Until someone blew it out." She eyeballed Rachel, who blushed instantly.

"Libby? A witch? You have to be joking, right?" I had to ask.

"Why? Because she doesn't have a wart on her nose or wear a black pointy hat? There are fewer things more dangerous than an unsatisfied witch. Do what I'm telling you, young lady. All will be well."

"Jan, I'm surprised to hear all this from you. I knew nothing about any of this. I mean, I knew we were weird, but this is totally weird!"

"Ha! You haven't heard anything yet. But that's for another time. Let's hear about your dreams, Carrie Jo. What have you seen?"

For the next forty-five minutes I told them everything I'd seen, from the attempted suicide of Tallulah to her actual demise. According to the records, not my dreams, she'd hanged herself in that same tree, the one that Trinket tried to talk her out of just a few days before. I told them about the tension between Aubrey and Percy, Percy's devastation over Tallulah's death and Bridget's utterly evil obsession with fairies.

"What about Michael?" Rachel asked me. "Have you dreamed about him?"

"Only in a peripheral way. When I dream about Trinket, I know that she is afraid of him. In fact, I wouldn't be surprised if he had something to do with her disappearance, but I can't be sure. In my most recent dream, Trinket found a letter from Aubrey to Tallulah. It warned Tallulah to marry Richard Chestnut and leave Idlewood, preferably before Percy and Aubrey returned. As unhinged as Tallulah was to begin with, that might have been just enough to push her over the edge. She could very well have taken her life because of that letter. It was cruel to say the least, and of course Percy knew nothing of it. He never found out, as far as we know." I chewed on the inside of my lip as I paced the room.

"So how do we help her? How do we help Trinket?"

"I think we have to do two things. Trinket wanted to prove that Tallulah's death was an accident because she didn't want her to be damned forever. Secondly, she wanted to acknowledge her sister and tell her she loved her. I think we help her by finding that letter or, if we can't do that, by telling her what happened and encouraging her to say Tallulah's name. Only by doing that will she free herself."

"And the man who pursues her? Is it Percy or Michael?" Rachel asked, her tired eyes puffy from the liquor.

"Personally, I don't think it's either one. I think the person who most wanted Trinket dead was Aubrey—she would never have wanted Percy to know what she'd done, and Trinket did know. He would always believe his Dot, that's what he called Trinket, over Aubrey. Always."

Suddenly Jan slapped her knees. "I'm tired and ready to go home. I'd like to sleep on all this and figure out a way to help. I can't let Rachel go back to that house without the proper protections, but I know she'll go with or without my permission." She patted her granddaughter's hand. "Let's do things the right way. Let Carrie Jo dream and see what she can see. Take my advice, though, CJ. Keep your husband home. He's in so much confusion right now that it would be hard for him to help. And he'd want to with all his heart."

"No problem. I think I can do that." I walked the women to the door and said goodnight to them.

As I turned off the music and the lights, I began to think about Trinket. I needed to see the letter. I needed to see that "magical place" where she'd hidden it.

Then and only then could we set her and her sister free, and maybe find her little body.

I walked up the stairs wearily, sadness overwhelming me. I didn't want to do this. I knew that tonight, after I closed my eyes, I would witness the death of a little child with sad eyes and sweet bow lips. A life cut short by someone who hated her enough to kill her and steal that life away from her.

I didn't bother changing clothes. Ashland was snoring, but I didn't care. I would sleep anyway. I cuddled up to his back and enjoyed the feeling of his breath rising and falling.

Rising and falling.

Rising and falling.

And suddenly, I was falling.

Chapter Eighteen—Trinket

My knee bled terribly, but I picked myself up from the dirty path and kept walking. Bridget was here somewhere in this tangle of trees, shrubs and flowers. This narrow trail led past the sunken garden and through a wild bramble of blackberry vines that had completely swallowed an abandoned corncrib. A rabbit bounced across the path in front of me, and for a moment I considered chasing after him. But I slid my hand into my pocket and remembered why I made this trip to begin with. There were no berries on the vines, it was still too cold for that, but they'd come in soon. The cascade of white flowers covering the abandoned building signaled that. Perhaps the bunny would have better luck finding a snack then and I could come back and see him, with Old Tramp, my favorite dog.

"Bridg-et!" I called into the trees just beyond. Better to let her know that I was on the way than to just show up and put myself in a precarious position. The Queen of the Fairies had a mean streak an acre wide, and it wouldn't do to upset her, not when I needed such a favor. I already dreaded hearing the price I would be forced to pay for asking, but the fear did not deter me. This was for Tallulah!

"Bridget, please! I need your help!" As if by magic, she stepped out from behind a tree.

"Why are you here, Trinket? I want to be alone."

"I know. I'm sorry, but I need your help. I need some…some magic."

Bridget folded her arms and peered down at me with her all-knowing dark eyes. She'd forgotten her flowery crown today, but there were leaves in her hair as if she had rolled in the grass. She wore a brown dress, nothing flamboyant or colorful like what she normally wore. She looked serious today. Not flighty at all. Just when I needed her to be. Just when I believed in her.

"You suddenly believe in magic?" She leaned against the tree, her hands behind her back now. I stole a peek at them. I saw no sharp knives, needles or hatpins. I swallowed and carried on.

"I need to hide something. I want you to help me, with your magic. It's for Tallulah."

"Our Golden Sister asked you to hide something?" She smirked at me, but at least she didn't remind me that Tallulah was dead.

"No, she didn't, but it could set her free, Bridget."

"What is it, and who are you hiding it from?" This entire conversation seemed strange. Bridget's serious demeanor disturbed me, but I couldn't stop now. I sighed and took a few steps toward her. I dug in my pocket and pulled out the letter. Bridget accepted it with a suspicious glance. I watched with trepidation as she read it. Who was to say she wouldn't destroy it? After a minute she folded it and slid down the tree, staring at me. "So you admit I have all the power? I have the power to set Tallulah free? You admit that and are willing to pay the price?" I nodded glumly and stared at my dirty black shoes. "I want to hear you say it, Trinket. No more running from me when I need your blood. You will give it to me when it is required, and you will always remember that *I* have all the power. You won't refuse me again?"

My rebellious soul did not want to agree with her. I didn't want to tell her what she wanted to hear. She was a cruel, hateful sister, but she was the only one I had left. Tallulah was gone from me. "You have all the power," I said as a fat tear landed on the top of my dusty shoe.

"And…"

"I won't refuse you. You can set Tallulah free." If only Percy had been at the house, but he was gone. He'd fled Idlewood after his argument with Aubrey. I had no doubt that even now my sister-in-law was tearing up the house looking for the evidence of her cruel betrayal.

Bridget took my hand, and I followed her, nearly tripping over my own feet. We walked through the woods, and a cold trickle of sweat ran down my back. To my surprise, she had made a house out of branches and stones. It was small, but there was a fire burning outside of the structure, and on the ground I noticed rabbit fur. I wondered what evil things she'd done here. Beyond the house was a small clearing, and I noticed tiny arrangements of furniture, tiny enough for Bridget's fairies.

"Are there fairies here?"

"Of course there are. Can't you see them?" she said snippily as she dug through a wicker basket of dried flowers.

"I'm trying," I said, squinting and staring as hard as I could. I thought I saw movement, but it was only a curious dragonfly. "I think I see something."

"You lie. They aren't here right now. They always hide when interlopers come near."

"I'm no interloper!" I shouted at her angrily. I wasn't sure what an interloper was, but I didn't like the sound of it.

"You dare argue with me after your pledge?"

"No, Bridget. I'm sorry." She handed me back the note. "Wait, aren't you going to help me?"

"Yes, I am. But you know the price." Then I noticed the small blade in her hand. She licked her lips as she stared at my fingers.

"Oh, wait." I pulled up my skirt and showed her the wound on my knee. The blood had flowed down into my sock. "Can't you use this? It's fresh."

With a delighted smile she slipped her knife in her pocket and reached for a small glass bottle. I recognized it as one of mother's old medicine bottles; she'd complained for weeks that someone had stolen it. She had been correct. There was already a dark liquid in the bottle, but Bridget squeezed my wound and forced a few drops of blood into the bottle as I yelped. Popping the cork in the bottle, she shook the liquid together and handed it to me.

"What do I do with this?" My nose crinkled as I frowned at the nasty-looking concoction.

"You drink it, idiot. Drink it and then hide the note wherever you like. The potion will give you the magical ability you need to cast the protection spell."

"Oh." I stared at the bottle again. "What do I say?"

She tapped the cleft in her chin and smiled. For the first time in a long time, it didn't make my skin crawl. Well, it wouldn't, would it? I was evil now too. I was making a pact with the Queen of the Fairies. "Let us find a good one." She went inside her makeshift hut and came back with one of her books. It had been a gift from our uncle. He'd encouraged her to read the books and often took her searching for fairies in the woods. I never liked our Uncle Preston. He never wanted to take me fairy hunting.

She flipped through the brittle yellow pages. She continued to search until she found the charm she wanted. "Here it is." She tapped on it. I tried to read it, but the writing was complicated and I could read only a few letters. We had not had a governess in over a year. Tallulah was to teach me, but she often forgot and I never reminded her.

"What does it say, sister?"

"You are stupid, aren't you? Don't tell me you can't read."

"I can so read. I read this letter, didn't I? But those letters are hard to read."

"That's because it is calligraphy, special writing for magic people. I will read it for you, but you must memorize it. Think about a hiding place. Tell no one where you will hide it. Hide the letter, drink the potion—it will give you power—and say the spell. The spell is good only once, though, and you must think of the item while you say it. Once you remove the letter from the hiding place, it won't be protected anymore."

"That's okay. I just want to hide it until Percy comes home," I said honestly, happy that she didn't call me stupid again.

"Okay, remember this spell. You must say it correctly. *Africanus objecticus, ublius shamara!*"

"What?" I said stupidly. She shook her brown head and tapped the spell with her dirty finger. It bothered me that her nails were dirty, as if she'd been digging in the earth. Mother would never approve.

"Say it with me, Trinket. *Africanus objecticus, ublius shamara!*" After about five times, I got it right. When she was satisfied, Bridget waved me away. "Now go. Cast your spell. Your letter will be safe, no matter where you hide it."

"And you're sure this will work?" She stood now, and her mood darkened quickly. "I'm sorry. I'm going. Thank you, Bridget. Sister. Queen of the Fairies!" I bowed a little to her. If this really worked, then she would truly be a magical creature and worthy of a good bow. She smiled now, showing her lovely dimples. Then she turned back to her business, and I ran home.

When I made it back to Idlewood, the place was in a stir. Aubrey was yelling at my mother; Michael, the servants and I were steering clear of the argument. I didn't understand the reason for their most recent disagreement, and I didn't want to know. Michael closed the door to the study. He stayed there quite often now, poring over Father's accounting books with Mr. Quigley, the attorney. Father's death had taken a toll on my brother. Any small amount of kindness within him died with our father. All he ever wanted was Father's approval. Now he would never receive it. Since Percy largely abandoned us so frequently, all the decision-making fell on Michael's shoulders. For many weeks Mother and Aubrey were forbidden to purchase dresses until Michael squared things away. Now that he had gotten a handle on the accounting, everyone was given an allowance. This irked Mother greatly, but what could she do about it? Father had left everything to his sons. Nothing for her at all, beyond Michael's generosity. Her Golden Son had turned his back on her, she bemoaned loudly. Now Michael alone received all her undying love and affection.

Anyone with a brain could see he did not want it. Not in the least.

I kept my eyes down and wandered back out of the house and to the kitchen with Mr. Lofton. He had fuzzy white eyebrows that looked like friendly caterpillars. He was sick today but still working hard. He twisted bread into the familiar shapes and prepared to bake them for supper. The day had escaped me. It was only an hour until dark, and my stomach was rumbling.

"Good evening, little miss. What's that you got there?" My hands flew in my pockets in a panic. I couldn't tell him about the potion, the spell and the letter! Then I realized he was talking about my knee. "Hop up here like a good girl, and I'll take a look at it." I climbed up on the chair and then the table. I pulled my linen dress up to show off my bloody knee. "That's a good'un. How did that happen? You aren't climbing trees, are you?"

Thoughts of Tallulah climbing and then swinging from the tree filled my head. "No, sir. I just tripped and fell."

"This might sting a bit, but you've got to clean it." He dipped a cotton towel in some water and handed it to me. "Here, you do it. You're too big, too much of a lady now, for me to be dabbing your knees for you."

"Aw," I said, feigning disappointment. I took the cloth and winced as I dabbed the dirt out. Mrs. Potts came in and scolded me for sitting on the table.

"You're not eating dough, I hope? That will make your belly swell as big as mine!" she joked pleasantly and pinched my cheek. "Now get down. We've got to bring supper up. Do yourself a favor, miss. Go get a bath and change your clothing before your mother sees you. She's on a tear today."

"Good idea." I tore off a piece of dough and popped it in my mouth before I ran from the kitchen, into the servants' entrance and upstairs to snoop around the house. The argument had died down by then, and everyone was dressing for dinner. I found an embroidery work in the sitting room. It captured my attention because it had a butterfly on it, but then I realized it was Aubrey's. I took a needle and pulled at the threads, making them uneven. *Hmph. That would teach her.*

Feeling a tiny bit of vindication, I went back to the room I now shared with the ghost of my sister. At least, I fancied that I did. In fact, last night I dreamed about her, but I couldn't remember what I had dreamed. This morning I tried for hours to recall her words, but to no avail.

Quietly I began thinking about where I would put the letter. Percy would be back soon, I hoped, but it could be days. It could be weeks. Since I had no way to write him, for I did not know where he went, this was my only option. Mother wouldn't care about the letter, and Michael wouldn't have time for such childish things. But I had to show Percy. He had to know the truth. Maybe he could help Tallulah, free her from purgatory, as I knew he would want to do.

I'd left my door open as I searched through my dresses. I heard the clock downstairs chiming the supper hour. It was seven o'clock! Where had the time gone? Michael would be very displeased. Uncaring that the door was wide open, I slid out of the dirty dress and slipped into the blue one. I'd never worn it before, but it looked much like all the others I had. A plain dress with a white pinafore and matching bow for my hair. As I pledged before, I didn't wear the bow. I slid the potion and the letter in my pocket, left off my stockings and put my feet in my slippers. I hoped Michael wouldn't notice them. He was a stickler for appearances.

I raced down the stairs and paused at the new clock. Why not here? Mrs. Potts had shown me the secret panel on the right side. She kept the clock's key there, but it wasn't scheduled to be wound for another month. This would be the perfect place to hide the letter. Seeing no one about, I squatted down, pushed on the panel and put my note inside. With another push, the panel popped back in place. I stared at the clock's face. *Okay, Mr. Clock, my sister's fate is in your hands. Please protect my letter.* I held the potion in my hand, but before I could drink it or repeat the magic spell, I heard my brother's angry voice calling me. Feeling conflicted, I left my secret in the clock and walked into the dining room.

I immediately regretted my decision. The five of them were there: Mother, Michael, Bridget (who looked remarkably cleaner), Aubrey and Mr. Quigley. "Where have you been?" Michael demanded.

"I am sorry. I lost track of time." I stared down at my slippers.

"Where is your bow, and when was the last time you brushed your hair?" my mother snarled as she sipped her evening claret.

"I brushed it this morning, and I'm too old for bows now, Mother."

"Hardly. You look a mess, Trinket. Why don't you go to your room and tidy up?"

Bridget grinned at me. I felt like she was trying to tell me something, but I had no idea what that might be.

"You will get no supper tonight, Trinket. Go to your room and go to bed. This will be a lesson to remember. I am sure if your father were here, he would agree with me."

"Father never sent me to bed without supper!" I said angrily.

Michael rose so quickly I thought his chair would fall over. "Leave now or I will strap you!" I knew he meant every word of it.

Tears filled my eyes. I had no one now. No Percy. No Tallulah. No Father. I was surrounded by people who hated me. Anger welled up in me, and I screamed as loudly as I could, "I hate you! I hate you all!" Michael was so surprised, he didn't run after me. I ran as fast as I could up the stairs. Tallulah's room was at the end of the hall. I wished, I prayed, I hoped I would find her there. I ran into the room, ignoring my mother's calls to return. I slammed the door with the full force of my anger and dragged a chair to put under the doorknob. Nobody could come in now. Nobody could correct my behavior with a strap or a tongue-lashing. They deserved it. They deserved to hear my wrath, my anger.

I flopped on my sister's bed and sobbed until I fell asleep.

When I woke, it was dark and raining. I slid off the bed, feeling sullen still. My stomach was rumbling loudly now. Maybe someone had left me a tray outside my door? I peered through the crack and saw no one. I moved the chair and carefully opened the door. There was no food. No glass of milk. I listened for sounds that anyone was awake, but nobody was. It was quite late now—the clock struck 11, and I knew I should be in bed. But I had an enchantment to finish. I went back in the room and returned the chair to its position. I couldn't be interrupted.

I felt the bottle in my pocket. I had to drink it and then speak the magic spell. Could I remember the spell now? What was it? Africanus...yes, that part I remembered. I paced the floor as the lightning cracked nearby. Suddenly I had perfect recall. *Africanus objecticus, ublius shamara!* Before I could forget again, I pulled the potion out of my pocket and drank it. It tasted foul, like sickly flowers, dirty mushrooms and some other things that I was sure I didn't want to properly identify, including my own blood. For a few seconds I felt the urge to vomit, but with some effort, I kept the potion down. This was worse than cod liver oil! But I couldn't lose the magic! I rolled on the floor, clutching my stomach until the urge passed. Once the nausea dissipated I stood up slowly and focused on breathing normally. I found myself in front of my sister's mirror. I did as Bridget told me. I thought about the hiding place and the letter and said the words loudly: *Africanus objecticus, ublius shamara!*

As I blinked in the darkness, the lightning illuminated my reflection in the mirror.

I was no longer myself! That wasn't my face looking back at me! I stepped closer to the mirror, and the other girl, the one who wasn't me, watched me curiously. She walked toward me too. She looked almost like me but not quite the same, I observed as the lightning continued to crack and the floor creaked under my footsteps. Her hair was darker, and she had dark eyes. She wore no bow in her hair; in fact, her hair was short. I liked the look of her short hair. I wished I could wear my hair short too.

"Who are you?" I asked the reflection, but then the image melted away and it was just me again. I waved my hands at myself and was surprised to see that light illuminated them. Bridget's magic had worked! I too had magical powers! Forgetting about the girl in the mirror for a moment, I turned to look at the world around me. It was exciting to see it in such a magical way. Everything seemed better, different, and my head felt as if it would float away, float right off my shoulders!

Somewhere in the distance, I heard someone crying. Must be Mother, crying for Tallulah. She cried for her Golden Daughter every night. But the girl in the mirror, where had she gone? I touched my hair. It felt heavy and sloppy, tangled like evil ropes around my head. But I had scissors, didn't I? I could cut my hair. I plundered Tallulah's sewing basket and found the heavy scissors there. Standing in front of the mirror, I began cutting my hair. I laughed as I lopped off the hair on the left, and then the hair on the right. I watched the clumps fall to the floor, and I felt free. I danced and spun, feeling lighter than I had ever felt, even lighter than I felt after prayers. I grabbed the hair at the back of my head and with some effort cut it off too. I let the scissors fall from my hand and stared at the pile of hair on the floor. The coils looked like brown snakes. They began to move like snakes too! I scurried to the bed and jumped on it, covering my face with a pillow. I stayed there for a while until I forgot what I had been afraid of.

Thunder rolled over Idlewood. It drew me to the window that overlooked the roof jutting out beneath it. I'd always loved this room. Tallulah's room. It was the only one without a balcony, but it had this sloped roof. When I was small, I often spied on Tallulah and Percy as they sat on the roof and looked at the stars. How close they'd been! How I loved them!

I heard someone knocking on my door. Perhaps it was Bridget calling me, but I couldn't be sure. She sounded more and more like Mother every day. I hated Mother. She had never wanted me. I was not golden enough. But I never hated Percy or Tallulah for their beauty. They loved everyone, especially one another. I slid the window open and let the rain beat on my face. It drenched me in a matter of seconds. I stuck my hands out the window, and they practically shone with light now. The magical power within me was getting stronger. But how long would it last? I had cast the protection spell, but was it enough?

No. It wasn't enough. I knew what I had to do.

I kicked off my slippers and slung my legs over the side of the windowsill. Bridget banged on the door. "Let me in, Trinket!"

"I have the power now, Bridget! I have it!" I called back as I stepped outside onto the wet roof. She would never get in here to stop me. The chair barred her way.

The rain came down harder now, or maybe it just felt that way because I had so much magic in me. Yes, I was bursting with it! Just like this thunder and lightning! I had to stand there, just at the edge. I had to stand above them all, and I had to say it! I had to say her name! I would no longer be afraid to speak her name, for she was my sister. If I could speak it, I would break the evil spell over her and she would be free, free to leave the place of the damned. Yes, that was all I had to do! And I was strong now. Strong enough to save her.

I inched toward the edge of the roof, closer still. Yes, I had to stand there. Just as I had in my dream! I put my arms out to my sides, as I'd seen Bridget do when she began her fairy dance. I was like a dancer now, full of magic and love for my Tallulah.

Now! Here! This was far enough! I had to do it! I opened my mouth to speak it out, but the words never came. Thunder shook the house, and I began to fall. I stared up into the dark sky as the lightning flashed again.

And then I was no more.

Chapter Nineteen—Carrie Jo

I woke with a sob. What a horrible thing! Poor Trinket! I gazed at the clock. It was five now, and Ashland slept soundly beside me. Baby AJ would be home in a few hours, and this wasn't going to wait. I grabbed my shoes and purse and slipped out of the house as I sent Rachel a text.

You up?

Yep. Haven't slept.

Meet me at the house. I know what we have to do.

Okay!

Since I lived closer to Idlewood, I arrived quite a while before Rachel did. I walked in the house, unafraid now. The sadness and seriousness of my dream hung over me like my own "magical" protective barrier. I walked to the clock, pushed open the panel and found the yellowed letter still hidden. With tears in my eyes, I carefully unfolded it and read the heartbreaking message, the one that likely sent Tallulah to her death and indirectly led to Trinket's death as well.

Rachel walked in and closed the door behind her. She rubbed her jacket sleeves and shivered. "Cold in here, but I don't feel anything negative now."

"That's because I know the truth. We know the truth. Look at this, Rachel."

She took the letter and read it. "It's just like you said. But what happened to Trinket?"

Rachel Kowalski…

"She's here!" she said.

"Don't be afraid. She won't hurt you. In fact, she saw you in her mirror a long time ago. She trusts you."

"What?"

"I don't have time to explain. For some reason, we have to do this now. She's upstairs, in Tallulah's room. Waiting for you. We have to go to her. I'll stay with you." She took my hand, and together we walked up the stairs. Thankfully, there was no stomping, no signs of Rachel's Shadow Man. We'd have to deal with him later, that much I knew. But today, this was about Trinket. She'd shown me what happened, and she was reaching out to us for help.

We stood outside the door of Tallulah and Trinket's room. For some reason, I knocked. And as if I expected it, a little girl's voice answered.

Come in...

I didn't know what Rachel could see, but as I swung the door open I saw the room as it used to be. The standing mirror, the four-poster bed, the rag rug made entirely of pink, red and purple rags. I saw the open window and the child, Trinket. The scissors were on the floor, and her hair lay in clumps. Rachel fell to her knees and sobbed. I touched her shoulder to reassure her. She took the letter out of her pocket and unfolded it.

"I found it, Trinket," she cried, the emotions overwhelming her. I felt them too, but not like Rachel did. Her sensitivity allowed her to pull emotions from everyone in the room, including Trinket. "And I'm going to tell the world the truth about what happened. Everyone will know the truth. I promise, Trinket. They will know."

The girl hovered by the window, which I saw was open now. She wasn't quite sure. She didn't quite believe.

"Call her Dot, Rachel. Tell her the magic worked."

"Okay," Rachel whispered to me. She clutched my hand and said, "Dot, the magic worked. It worked perfectly."

Trinket laughed and spun before us, changing into a misty cloud. Then she slipped out the window. I ran after her to watch. The small spirit walked out on the roof, and I could see her still hovering, the sun threatening to rise in the distance. I felt such an urgency—it had to happen now. Rachel was beside me staring at the girl, her dress wet, her hair shorn sloppily, her skin pale. The child raised her arms as if she believed she could fly. I heard Rachel whimper beside me. "No, it's okay. She's not going to jump. She never jumped. She fell. But now it's time. Tell her, Rachel. Tell her now is the time. She has to say her name now!"

In a rush, Rachel repeated what I told her, "Now is the time, Dot! Say her name now!"

Arms still outstretched, Trinket looked at us once more and then turned her eyes to the far horizon, smiling at the sun's first rays.

"Tallulah Ferguson! I remember you! I love you! I will never forget you!" As she spoke, Trinket began to fade, her arms waving like a dancer's as she spun around happily.

With one last breath before she vanished, I heard her whisper, "Thank you."

Rachel fell into my arms and cried as she clung to me. "Now I remember. Now I remember. I did see her. I saw her in the mirror, but I thought I dreamed it. She was always with me. Just waiting until I made it here. All these years."

"And here you are, and I am so happy you're here." Together we walked out of the house, leaving the ghosts of Idlewood behind.

At least for a little while.

Epilogue—Carrie Jo

Magical hardly described the wedding of Detra Ann Dowd and Henri Devecheaux. It was honest and sweet, but not in an immature way. Painted white trees covered with hundreds of twinkling fairy lights decorated the walkways to the ballroom, which someone had cast in enchanting lavender light. A string quartet played now, but after the traditional dances, a jazz band would take the stage and the sounds of New Orleans would bounce through the rooms of Seven Sisters. Perhaps the ghosts wouldn't mind too much.

Maybe that meant good magic was at work here. Even the kiss, which was highly anticipated by some, was just plain right. They'd done it! And they were going to be fine.

Detra Ann looked a dream in her fitted white gown with the low bustle. At the back of her neat updo she wore a smaller pouf of white fabric. She was the most beautiful bride I'd ever seen. And the happiest. But then, why shouldn't she be? She'd helped her Harry find his lost cousin. And to think, she'd been near their old house in Dumont the whole time.

Aleezabeth Eileen Devecheaux's bones were recovered at last. She'd been buried in a shallow grave at the back of Henri's grandmother's property. He couldn't believe it, since the area had been searched so thoroughly when she went missing. The current theory was that she'd been kept alive for a while before she was killed and buried, but who really knew? And although Trevor Devecheaux had been questioned, there were still no solid answers about what happened to Aleezabeth. Even the coroner was unsure. After Henri and Detra Ann's honeymoon, the four of us were traveling to Dumont, and I was scheduled to spend the night in the old homestead. It was our wedding gift to our best friends. At least Ashland no longer saw Aleezabeth.

Ashland and I clapped for the quartet, and Henri turned and gave us a thumbs-up. Ash turned his attention to the crowd, but I didn't think he saw any of their faces. I suspected he was searching the room for invisible visitors. During the cake cutting ceremony, he whispered to me, "Mostly the living."

"They are at rest now."

"I hope so." He kissed my neck and whispered in my ear, "Muncie is here. I wish you could see him. He looks different, but I know it's him. Same eyes, same expression. And she's here too. Calpurnia. They are together but always apart now. I feel sadness between them, but I don't understand it."

The musicians played a slow song, and the serious mood vanished. I glanced at the sea of faces. Angus was bringing Rachel a glass of champagne, and Chip sulked not far away. He'd brought a date, but she was old enough to be his mother. I felt sorry for the guy but happy for Rachel. Angus? The jury was still out on him. Ashland smiled at me with his easy, college-boy grin and pulled me out of my people-watching. Such a flirt, and I loved every minute of it. Still I couldn't help but feel that things were brewing.

"Something is about to happen, Ash. You ready for whatever lies ahead?"

"Something is *always* about to happen! It's Mobile! And whatever it is, we will be fine. At least Libby's seen the light and dropped her lawsuit. Although I don't know why."

"Because she's a liar, plain and simple. And on that note, Mr. Stuart..." I took my plate and tossed it on a nearby table. I giggled like a teenager as I practically dragged him from the ballroom to the Blue Room. We'd miss a few of the "first" dances, but I was in the mood for a first of my own. It was cool here in the Blue Room and surprisingly free of ghosts, shades, wraiths.

That was nice. And rare here in the old house.

Then I was lost in the wonderful warmth of Ashland's arms, the smell of him on my skin, the laughter of guests in the other room, the tinkling of glasses as the toasts began. They'd be wondering where we were, not thinking at all that we were making love in the room where it all began.

It was good to be home again.

Read more from M.L. Bullock

The Seven Sisters Series

Seven Sisters
Moonlight Falls on Seven Sisters
Shadows Stir at Seven Sisters
The Stars that Fell
The Stars We Walked Upon
The Sun Rises Over Seven Sisters

The Idlewood Series

The Ghosts of Idlewood
Dreams of Idlewood (forthcoming)
The Whispering Saint (forthcoming)
The Haunted Child (forthcoming)
The Heart of Idlewood (forthcoming)

The Desert Queen Series

The Tale of Nefret
The Falcon Rises
The Kingdom of Nefertiti
The Song of the Bee-Eater (forthcoming)

The Sugar Hill Series

Wife of the Left Hand
Fire on the Ramparts (forthcoming)
Blood by Candlelight (forthcoming)

To receive updates on her latest releases,
visit her website at MLBullock.com
and subscribe to her mailing list.

CPSIA information can be obtained
at www.ICGtesting.com
Printed in the USA
LVOW13s1947051117
555097LV00040B/1380/P